PRAISE FOR HIDING LIES

"It's hard to believe *Hiding Lies* is Stephanie Rose's first book, as it reads like the work of a surefooted veteran. Fans of Caroline Kepnes and Thomas Harris will be thrilled with this twisty novel anchored by a pair of vividly-drawn narrators."

-Nick Cutter, national bestselling author of *The Troop*

"No surprise that horror maven Stephanie Rose had such a killer novel up her sleeve! *Hiding Lies* is brutal, unrelenting, and pitch-black from start to finish. I read the whole thing eyes covered and jaw dropped. Rose exposes every dark aspect of humanity swiftly and unapologetically and gives us the scariest duo I've seen in fiction yet!"

-CJ Leede, author of *Maeve Fly* and *American Rapture*

"Stephanie Rose has come out of hiding with this undeniably thrilling debut. A disturbing cat and mouse tale with the ferocity of your favorite Hannibal episode, *Hiding Lies* will set up camp in the shadows of your psyche long after the final breathtaking page is turned."

-Brian McAuley, author of *Candy Cain Kills* and *Curse of the Reaper*

"There is a darkness at the core of *Hiding Lies* that seeps out from its pages, thicker than blood, as pitch black as the Portland woods at midnight. One can't help but feel as though it stains their fingers, their eyes, their very soul. Tread carefully through this brutal book. It marks you."

-Clay McLeod Chapman, author of *What Kind of Mother* and *Ghost Eaters*

"Dark, disturbing, and twisty ... What more could you want from a serial killer novel? Stephanie Rose's debut novel is a wicked cat-and-mouse game that will keep you up late reading ... and maybe looking over your shoulder."

-Samantha Downing, internationally bestselling author

"*Hiding Lies* is equal parts twisted and addictive. Once I began reading, I devoured this book until its satisfying and disturbing end."

-Steph Nelson, author of *The Final Scene* and *The Vein*

Hiding Lies

Stephanie Rose

Mad Axe Media

Published by Mad Axe Media

madaxemedia.com

Edited by Joey Powell

Book Cover by Joey Powell

Print ISBN: 979-8-9891730-2-0

E-Book ISBN: 979-8-9891730-3-7

Hiding Lies contains content that some readers may find disturbing, including sexual assault, domestic abuse, child abuse, child death, and mentions of animal abuse.

To Ken, my partner who has always encouraged me to be my spooky self,
and to all of those who identify as strange and unusual. Embrace it.

Chapter 1

LYDIA

I think about death more than I'd ever admit. Sometimes I think about ending my own life, but I've never acted on it. I have this one fantasy when I'm driving: I cut the wheel so sharp to the left that I smash into the freeway median. Occasionally, while I'm on a long and winding country road, surrounded by breathtaking mountain views, I think about pressing the gas pedal all the way down and driving off a cliff. There would be a moment of complete bliss, where all I would hear would be the whirring of the wind. I imagine admiring the scenery all the way down. The trip would be unforgettable. Some people think that suicide is weak, but I find it almost admirable. There's bravery in pulling a trigger, in slitting your wrist, in swallowing a handful of pills.

Sometimes my violent thoughts will turn on others. Someone will give me a particularly nasty look while I'm walking down the street, or a reckless driver will nearly hit me in traffic and I'll immediately think of five or six ways I could kill them. A woman could step in front of me in line at the bank and I'd think of squeezing her pretty little neck until all the breath was out of her. Walking through the park, I see a mother slap her child. Some parents are so vile. At once, I'm fishing my hand in my jeans pocket, playing with the sleek blade of my folding knife. I should use the knife to play with this abusive bitch instead. I imagine taking my time and sticking it lightly into all different parts of her arms and stomach. Then I could straddle her and dig my thumbs right into her eyes, blinding her from the life that she takes for granted.

It's a struggle to not act on these impulses. I'm consumed by memories from a time when desperate action was all that was left to me. So now I surround myself with murder in my leisure. I read true crime accounts and countless crime thrillers. I must have read and watched *The Silence of the Lambs* over a hundred times. There's something poetic, even romantic, about the way Thomas Harris creates a killer. You can't help but respect the cannibal and empathize with the FBI trainee.

I pursued a career where I can be surrounded by true sociopaths and by the brutalized bodies they leave behind. I work as a forensic photographer and I'm a teacher's assistant in a forensic sciences program downtown. It's not that I don't feel bad for the victims of violent crimes, but I respect the killers' work even more. My job affords me intimate contact and privileged information, it's the closest I can get to walking in the footsteps of a killer. I believe that the devoted murderer is an artist and that his victims are a medium of expression. Even if you don't understand it, you have to appreciate the vision. I've always been interested in photography, and I love the way I'm able to peer through a lens and see a snapshot of a person's life. With a camera in hand, I can keep a barrier between myself and other people, I can still get close without ever letting them in, and often without them even knowing I'm looking. As my fascination with true crime grew, I decided to study forensic science. I wanted a career where I could work around people, but not necessarily with them.

I've never been able to trust anyone. I've felt disconnected, in one way or another, throughout my life. I hoped things would get better after moving to Portland. I made a few friends while waiting tables and I've been asked out on a couple of dates but none of it ever went anywhere. I always come across as too eager or too aloof. I can't just be me. I'm quiet and it takes me longer to recharge and friends and boyfriends tend to take that as me blowing them off. But I like staying in. I love my apartment. It's my comfy sanctuary. Because for the first time I have somewhere safe to live.

As a child, I wasn't exposed to the outside world as often as most people. It's loud and scary, and people irritate me with how little regard they have for each other. The other day I felt so closed in at the grocery store. The early evening crush of bodies had me on edge as I was jostled in narrow aisles and my cart was repeatedly crashed into. My heartbeat thundered in my ears loudly as I swore that I'd never shop again at prime time, never again before night, the later and more desolate the better. You'd feel that way too if, as a child, you had been locked in a closet night after night. To this day I'll sometimes wake up confused and curled up in my closet or on the bathroom floor, I'll spend the quiet hours of the night pressing my cheek against the cool, still, porcelain bathtub. I never remember how I got there. That's probably one of the reasons I can't seem to keep a boyfriend. I don't know how I'd react if I woke up to find that the man I was dating had left our bed to sleep on the floor by himself.

I was a foster child from a very young age, so I guess that settles it. When you're little you're supposed to be able to trust your parents unconditionally, my parents gave me away. They decided that their lives would be better off without the child they had created. I still don't understand why my mother didn't just have an abortion. It would have been easier for her and a hell of a lot easier for me.

My childhood was a blur. I was brought in to many foster families and each was friendly at the start, but eventually they would turn against me. After a few months—six was the record—I would become an unwelcome guest in their home. Being thrown around like that felt like being driven through a dark tunnel, occasionally and suddenly bursting into the light. Each new family was a patch of light that would dim all too quickly and I would be rushed back into darkness. In a new home, I would always follow the rules, no matter how contrived. It wasn't just the rules though, I needed to adjust to a whole new routine every few months, and daily life was more challenging and terrifying with every new house. No matter how bad things were I never complained, I thought it was all normal. With one of the families, I thought it was normal to be trapped at home alone, imprisoned in a closet day and night. I was let out three times a day for one hour at a time. At the beginning of each week, I was given two batteries for a tiny flashlight and a few books to keep in the closet.

"What do I do if the batteries die?" I asked in the way any child would ask with a fear of the dark.

"You'll have to wait until next week to get more, so use them wisely," he said, as he shut the door on my soft sobs. I cried myself to sleep that night and woke up with the realization that the whole thing, the life I had been dealt, was horrible and nightmarish.

At the age of eight, I didn't think twice when my foster parents told me that I'd be home-schooled. I was only allowed outside of the house under the strictest supervision and usually for less than an hour a day. I didn't even know what homeschooling was so I couldn't realize that I wasn't getting the education I deserved.

One foster family tried to make a business out of us. They found that they could trim down the costs of childcare to a bare minimum and still cash in on the monthly checks from the state. They gave us one meal a day and the rest of the time the refrigerator was double padlocked. My foster brothers and sisters would eat the meal greedily, but I took my time. I wanted to savor every bite of food and every moment of our time in the dining room before being locked back in the dank basement. Each of us had an old twin mattress laid directly on the ground. The basement floor was bare earth, so our feet were as black as coal, and our mattresses were streaked with grime. Every few months, the state would come around to check on us. On those days, our "caregivers" would take the locks off the doors and the fridge and make up some rooms upstairs. We got baths then and everything was touted up until the place was picture-perfect. I always wished we'd get more visitors, those were the best times. Of course, we couldn't complain. We all knew that if someone so much as spoke out of turn, we all would have been beaten or starved. So we played our parts, and the bastards got to keep their racket going for a time.

Sometimes I'll find myself in my kitchen in the middle of the night opening and shutting the refrigerator just because I can. The light from it illuminates my face and I am taken back to those days of light and dark. I brush my teeth in the middle of the day for no reason, and I'll occasionally lurch out of bed at 3:45 am to take a shower. I revel in these little displays of control because they remind me that I am not the helpless child I once was.

I want to let someone in but if they get too close they may discover my flaws and my dependence on these little rituals. These quirks aren't meant for anybody else. Usually, it's too much for people to handle. Maybe I'm not meant for anybody else and maybe I'll always be alone. How much of me is built on this faulty foundation?

I let my guard down once with a foster family. It was the last foster family that I ever lived with. The Carlson family had a daughter, Heather. She was younger than I was, and they were so excited to have me, but I wasn't so sure about them. I was really excited at the idea of having a little sister. But I had been discarded, abused, and neglected for so long that I was wary. I was twelve, so my foster care worker took my opinion into account and told me that it was my choice whether or not I wanted to be adopted. I would live with them for a while before deciding.

After a few months, I grew comfortable and the household routines sank in. I consented to the arrangement, I would stay with these people. That's when the nightly visits started. My foster father, Jacob, was a long-haul driver and he hadn't been home much those first few months. But I had already learned to avoid him whenever he was home since he was usually drunk. At least he was gentle and quick when he forced himself on top of me. I squeezed my eyes so tight that they ached. I eventually learned to think of a secluded place where no one could hurt me. I imagined a safe space full of trees, rivers, and waterfalls. I imagined the wind whistling through branches, and water crashing on the rocks. My imaginary forest became magnificent over time. I would retreat there and imagine new tracts of land while he abused me. It was somewhere I could escape to, my safe haven in my head. And there was ample time for the forest to grow.

I don't go to bars often but whenever I do I'm reminded of the whiskey smell on his breath. The morning after he first violated me, my foster mother, Beth, told me gravely that this was the only way she could keep her family together. This was the only thing she could do to keep him away from their daughter. She was too scared to tell anyone or to leave him. Her daughter was just about to turn nine... I could taste bile in the back of my throat and feel my skin crawl as the tremors came on. Suddenly I knew the fucked up reason for my adoption.

It wasn't because she wanted to help a girl who had no family, it was because she wanted to save her daughter. It only took a few months of seeing his footsteps in the light just beyond my door and hearing the doorknob turn with the faintest creak before I decided it was enough. I couldn't physically escape at the time but mentally and emotionally I did. He could have my body, but he couldn't take my mind or spirit. And to think I had been so excited to be given my very own room for the first time. It went on for two years until I had finally had enough. I still remember standing outside of the blazing house, I wasn't sorry.

I hear the rain outside my apartment in southeast Portland. I love this location. It's soothing to be tucked away a block from the hustle and bustle of Division Street. The rain masks the neighborhood noises, giving it the illusion of peace. I can leave my windows open during the day and all I hear is the drumming of the rain on the sidewalk, a wind chime making music in the distance, and birds singing and squawking. Looking out of my window I can see leaves dancing on the unforgiving wind. It's so hard to be certain what time of day it is because of the almost constant gloom. But the overcast sky suits me. Some days the sun teases its way through the clouds if only for a few minutes at a time. That's how hope feels. It's there one second and then it fades away, without any hint of when it will return.

My alarm went off a few minutes ago. I've been lying in bed listening to the rain for hours. Usually, I never sleep more than a few hours at a time. Of course today I forgot to shut off the alarm, on the only day that I don't have to be up early. I was looking forward to a lazy Saturday with my cats. I feel like one of my cats sometimes, except that I have to take all of my naps in one go. I try to stay as busy as possible to keep my mind distracted and in the present, but still, I do welcome a day at home.

I lie on my bed staring out the window slowly closing and opening my eyes. My cell phone buzzes on the nightstand, and I reluctantly wrench the pillow beneath my chin so I can squint my sleepy eyes at the screen. It's Frank. I rarely get calls this early on the weekend, there has to be a new case. Fumbling with excited fingers, I snatch my phone and press answer.

"Walker here," I say.

I know it's your day off," Frank says, his voice shaky. "Can you come in this morning? A couple has been discovered brutally murdered... found by a hiker in Norton."

I jolt up in bed. In the five years that I've been working with the Portland Police Bureau, we haven't once been called in on anything from outside our county. This must be a gruesome case. Frank doesn't even give me a chance to consider.

"It sounds pretty bad," he continues. "The couple was stabbed to death while they were on a camping trip. Local officials haven't done much with the crime scene yet. They want photographs of everything before they go ahead. They said they've never seen anything like this, so be prepared. They've even called in the FBI. You might be able to work the investigation from their side too."

"When can you be here?" I say, already out of bed and tearing through my closet, snatching a pair of black pants, a white silk button-up blouse, and a black blazer.

"I was hoping you'd say that. I'm already on the way. Be ready." And with that, the line goes dead.

I'm more than ready. For years I tried to fight my feelings of admiration for these killers. Lately, I've given up on fighting. I've been waiting for a case like this, and with the FBI getting involved at this early stage, I have no idea what to expect. Though I'd never admit it to anyone, I almost hope they don't catch the killer, at least for a while. Anyone who's never been treated like property might believe I'm sick to think optimistically about a case like this, but focusing on the violent experiences of others allows me to bury memories of my own brutal past. I would love to follow this thing through to its conclusion—a case that's bound to be more exciting than the normal fare. Lately, all of our cases have been cut and dry.

Frank Morris has been a detective with Portland for almost two decades. I've worked with him on a few cases over the last five years. He's my favorite detective at the precinct because he doesn't pry. Since I work as a forensic photographer, I get to keep to myself most of the time, which I love. Frank never asks me if I'm alright. He knows not to bother me when I'm lingering around a crime scene, and oftentimes I wonder if he notices how mesmerized I become by the carnage laid bare before the lens. But I can be myself around Frank, and he doesn't mind when I'm quiet. Sometimes we talk shop about the cases, and sometimes we just sit together in silence.

Looking into the bathroom mirror, I bow my head and throw my long black hair into a messy bun. Circling the reflection are the crime scene photographs I've collected over the years, my opportunity to capture and recreate the most intimate details of a crime. These portraits comfort me. The dead are the only ones you can really trust. These victims and their killers swim around my head. They give me something to focus on, something to distract me from my past.

We all have our distractions. I just need mine to be extra-strength.

One photograph hanging by my mirror is an extreme close-up of a woman. Her head rests on a pale gray shoulder, with crystal-blue eyes that are open but ever so slightly unfocused. At first, it's difficult to make out the blue, her pupils are obscured by the milky swirl of the newly opaque corneas. Those eyes are staring at me, without anger and without pretense. She had been brutally raped and murdered. She was left in a ditch in the middle of autumn, somewhere off the I-5. The eyes have begun to flatten, they sink to the back of the sockets, like old, bruised grapes set in an ashen bowl. All around her are leaves, covering her hair and framing her face. It's as if she's looking into the distance behind me, across my bedroom, and out at the street, she's finally at peace in this moment.

This is just one of the countless photographs on display. They're not just on the bathroom mirror, but in the living room as well. They hang on the wall opposite my couch and in the kitchen above the stove. I've stuck some of the newer ones to the fridge with magnetic poetry. My favorites are plastered all over my bedroom ceiling. Of these, one photograph is tacked up prominently in the center of the arrangement, directly above my bed. It's the last thing I see before I fall asleep, and it's what I awake to.

A five-year-old girl had been drowned by her mother in the bathtub. I composed the photo moments after she was pulled from the tub and laid onto the bathmat. Caramel strands of hair are matted against her cheeks and forehead like viscous veins. Her lifeless eyes are devoid of any rich colors, but they seem to stare straight into my lens, beads of water glitter as they cling to her eyelashes. She's wrapped in a daisy print towel, and her thin lips hold an expression of perpetual sadness. Bright plastic bath toys shout from the edge of the tub. The girl lay in a pool of water-stained pink. According to the forensic pathologist, the girl had gouged her scalp on the bathtub faucet, probably struggling to steal one last breath.

The door buzzer rings and brings me back to reality. I grab my coat and head out. As I step into the elevator I stare up into its mirrored ceiling, its reflection makes my face appear distorted. For once the way I look on the outside matches the way I feel on the inside.

Chapter 2

LYDIA

With my hood up, I take the stairs two at a time into the quiet Portland morning. It's the end of summer and finally time for fall, my favorite season. Lately, I've been hearing people on the street complaining about the cold or wishing the rain away. But I'll take it all, the fall foliage, Halloween, the nice cool mornings, and the drizzle. It's been unseasonably cold the last few weeks though. Not that September is usually a month of heat waves or anything. With the nearly constant rains and the bleak skies, the seasons kind of bleed together. Sure, summer is distinctive, but it only lasts a few minutes. I may be one of the few people who are ready for summer to be over as soon as it begins. There are always lots of people wandering the streets in summer, even very early in the morning. I guess people will try and make up for the eleven months of dreariness any way they can. This time of year, we start to get a break from the staggering clusters of day trippers that fill the sidewalks and hog the bike lanes. It's going to be nice to reclaim parts of the city I haven't dared explore since March.

I climb in the passenger side of Frank's sedan, and he starts speeding away before I can even get my seat belt on. As he drives off, he pulls a case file from the back seat and drops it on my lap. No time for pleasantries today. Frank's a stocky little man who always seems angry about something. It almost makes me laugh the way he's constantly muttering under his breath. I can never quite make out what the hell he's saying, but I like to think it's profane. I'm sure that if I had worked twenty years as a detective, I would be jaded too.

"The victims, Eric Black and Kasey Hill, were found this morning. It appears that they may have been killed as recently as this past weekend or as early as a week ago. We won't know until after the coroner's report. Local law enforcement and the FBI are participating in a media blackout on this one. So far, we're operating without leads."

It's more challenging to secure a crime scene when it's outside, especially when members of the press are trolling around. They'll listen in on police scanners and monitor cruiser dispatch patterns so they can move around the edges of a crime scene with long-range glass attached to their cameras to get shots of the forensics team in action. It's a smart move to keep them in the dark, at least for now.

"Where in Norton were they found?" I ask.

"Near the Halt Reservoir, also known as Norton Lake. It's a campsite in the Upper Lane Creek Campground. There are five campsites, very remote and very densely forested. I'm not surprised it took a while for them to be found. It's not a very popular spot since it's so far south of Portland. But this *is* the time of year for us to get overwhelmed by tourists. It seems some of them are reaching this far out of the metro. That's definitely going to put some pressure on us. We'll need this investigation resolved fast before the press gets a chance to scare people. According to their report, local police believe that before the hikers stumbled onto the scene, the victims may have been out there for days, rotting like pieces of old fruit."

The case file reveals no photographs of the scene. Usually, the first officer on the scene will take some pictures, or snap a few photos with a cellphone at the very least.

"You said it was pretty gruesome, but even so, it's strange that there wasn't a single photograph taken of the scene before our arrival." I want to get to the heart of why I'm here. "Why were Portland PB and the FBI called in before any forensics were done?"

"Portland PB told them you were the best forensic photographer around, and the locals wanted to wait. They're really afraid this is going to get out to the press. The officer in charge of the case called us and the FBI. Hopefully we have a shot to solve this a lot quicker together than the locals could by themselves. We need to catch this guy."

"Could be a girl," I say, watching streams of rain dance along the passenger window.

"Or girl," Frank says, wincing slightly. "But, statistically speaking, we can be pretty sure this was done by a man, especially if it's just the start of something. This area hasn't seen a crime this gruesome since Ted Bundy."

"Norton is a little over two hours from here," he says. "We'll grab coffees from Mugshots and I can fill you in on the case along the way. "In the years I've known Frank, he's never gone a day without stopping at this coffee shop, it's usually out of our way, but that's never stopped

Frank. He told me once that he started coming here because he liked the name. He thought it was appropriate for a cop to get his coffees from a place called Mugshots. It kept him optimistic that he would find his suspect. That he'd "get their mugshot."

He was married for a time but has been divorced for years. He was a big family man, loved his daughter so much. He was devastated when his daughter was killed. These days he lives for the job, like he's only at home on a case or at the station.

It took Frank over a year to tell me what had happened to his daughter, Dana. She had just received an undergraduate degree in psychology and had planned to go to graduate school in the fall. The summer she was killed she decided to take a cross-country trip from Portland, Oregon, to Portland, Maine. "She loved the idea of the sister cities," Frank had told me.

Frank was against the idea of Dana traveling by herself. "But she was twenty-three and headstrong," he'd told me with a wistful smile on his face and lingering pain in his dark eyes. "She couldn't be talked out of it."

Her naked body was discovered in a ditch off of I-80 outside of Omaha. She was sexually assaulted and tortured before she was murdered. It's been years since she was killed, but they still haven't caught her murderer. After a day of working his active caseload, Frank usually retires to the cot made up at the back of his office in the station. And when he can't sleep, he flips open Dana's file. That will be his life until he finds the killer or until Frank himself is in the ground.

We pull into a big parking lot swarmed with cop cars, some marked and some unmarked. All of the cars are centered around one car in the distance. It must have been the couple's rental car. Caution tape dangles from the mirror of the nearest cruiser, it stretches away from us and loops around a spruce tagged with a faded blue blaze. The trail starts just beyond. We get out and I grab my gear: film camera, digital camera, pen, notepad, position markers, and evidence identification.

We walk down a narrow trail with dead wet leaves matted to the ground. Downed branches fill the overlapping troughs made by the cruiser tires. The short trail opens up to a large circle of campsites with tall trees all around. It's impressive how large and secluded each of the five appear to be. I went camping once when I was a kid. Our campsite was almost on top of its neighbors. What I can see of this plot is three times the size of your garden variety campsite and most of it is still obscured by trees. Even at this point along the path, I can't tell if anyone's home. It's easy to see how the couple went unnoticed. The whole campground is right off of a road, but this road is almost exclusively used by loggers. No one just wanders into this camp. I can't see the bodies, but I'm ready.

At the edge of the campsite, my steps are halted. A tall, thin man with sandy blond hair and blue eyes is standing in front of me. His gray suit matches the clouds above us and a black tie hangs loose around his neck. It screams FBI. But it doesn't do much to hide his physique, and I'm pretty sure the FBI has mandated a ton of gym time for this guy.

"You must be the forensic photographer from Portland PB." He says this abruptly.

"That's me," I say, trying to contain my annoyance at being held up. "And you are?"

"Harshaw. It's Agent Michael Harshaw, FBI." A smug grin comes over his face. "The local PD asked for the FBI, and now I'm here."

"I was asking Frank earlier why they felt the need to call you in so quickly. It's a double homicide, not a series of murders."

"I think you'll understand once you become familiar with the crime scene. We hope this is an isolated incident, but I'm not so sure. And after looking at your portfolio, I'd love for you to work exclusively on this case until it's solved. I've already talked to Portland PB and they said they can spare you for a time, if that's alright with you," he explains, with a newly respectful tone in his voice.

Holding back my excitement, I look around pensively and take a deep breath before I respond. "So you really think it's a serial killer?"

"I didn't say that," Agent Harshaw insists.

"No, but that's the inference." I counter. "That is, if I'm needed on this one case *for a time,* there's either much more to this one scene than the file led me to believe, or you think there's going to be more bodies."

Anything to get me off of local duty. I've photographed enough dead prostitutes and robbery victims to last a lifetime. I've only dealt with a handful of cases that captured my attention, and this one seems like it might be truly interesting.

His eyes darting beyond me, Harshaw checks out the path behind where Frank is standing. I'm pretty sure he's looking to see if there's anyone in earshot. He moves a few steps closer to me and I can smell coffee and cigarettes on his breath.

"Look, no one in the FBI wants to say the word 'serial' out loud, but they definitely want to be prepared in case there's an uptick of similar scenarios in this general area. The agents back in D.C. in the Behavioral Analysis Unit will be working on a criminal profile for this one after they receive the crime scene information and all the photographs you take today. If it isn't a standalone double homicide, the need for a profile on the offender will be escalated." Harshaw takes a moment to straighten his tie before his eyes return to me. "Bottom line is that even with just this one double homicide, there are definitely indications that this may be the start of something."

We start walking. Harshaw is ahead of me, moving in on the crime scene, he keeps glancing back every few paces to make sure we're still behind him.

"One more question, at least for now," I say, staring at the collar of his jacket. "Were there any photographs in particular that impressed you in my portfolio?"

He stops dead in his tracks but doesn't make a move to turn back toward me.

"That's kind of an odd question," he announces over his shoulder.

"Never mind," I say, regretting that I asked.

For once I wish someone would hide their confusion and embarrassment from me. Or, better yet, I wish I could come across someone who was neither confused nor embarrassed whenever I make an off-the-cuff remark. It's too much, always being the odd one. It may prove to be impossible to find someone as dark as me, someone with an ugly morbid side.

I'm so afraid of letting anyone get close to me because they always pull away. I say too much about death and I talk too much about true crime. I can contemplate the different ways of murdering someone over coffee, but I probably shouldn't share those insights during a latte date. That's probably oversharing. If I even get remotely close to exposing my deepest darkest thoughts, people run the other way. I could see myself inviting someone over to my place, but I'd probably forget to take down the damn crime scene photographs. My dream companion would have to embrace these sides of me, not recoil away.

"The hiker found them right over here at this campsite," says Harshaw as he gestures to a plot a few feet forward and looks down at a case file. "He was pretty startled. He thought they were alive until he got close enough that he could see their faces. I think the guy is a little traumatized."

This didn't make sense at first. They said the couple had been dead for a few days at the very least.

But then I saw for myself.

A green four-person tent pitched a few feet from the fire pit of the campsite. Two camping chairs only inches apart with the armrests overlapping slightly. The back of a woman's head peaks over the back of one chair, resting on the shoulder of the body in the chair next to her. Their hands are intertwined.

I make my way closer, eyeing the ground that's been stained dark from the pool of blood surrounding their feet. Both victims are fully clothed, wearing rain jackets zipped to the neck. If it weren't for rigor mortis, they couldn't have stayed in these positions, propped against one another. It's clear from the state of the chairs and their clothes that they were killed elsewhere in the campsite and relocated shortly after death.

Kasey Hill's eyes have sunken considerably, and they are the faded green of a disused traffic signal. No light shines from behind her deflated irises. Her lids have been forced open, and she's staring straight ahead. She looks through me, like I'm not even here. Her blood-soaked copper hair lies against her shoulders underneath the black raincoat. Eric Black has a dark, well-kept beard, brown eyes, and shaggy brown hair underneath the dark blue hood of his slicker.

Gathered around me are the detectives, CSI unit, medical examiner, and Frank. After I've fully documented the immediate scene, the medical examiner carefully unzips the jackets of both victims. The collection of officers and forensic specialists gasp as the bodies are exposed. I hold my composure in the face of the carnage, but the silence that surrounds me is thick and lingering. Taking a small step forward, I'm not able to look away from her torso and dozens of visible knife wounds, I focus and snap another photo.

"There have got to be twenty-to-thirty knife wounds in her chest alone," the medical examiner says, bringing his ballpoint pen within three millimeters of a small slit in her flesh. "From this wound in the neck, it looks like he stuck the blade in at different amounts. At times he would stab her with only a quarter of the blade, and other times he would have stuck the knife all the way to the hilt. I'll know more back at the morgue."

Between snapping shots and making adjustments to the settings on my cameras, I call out to Frank and Agent Harshaw, "He moved the bodies." I can't take my eyes away from the victims. I scratch out notes blindly and drive position markers into the soil without breaking my morbid gaze.

"The local PD picked up on that too, it's hard to say how long he was actually with the victims. We found multiple chloroform-soaked rags left by the tent. It could be that he killed them over there." Harshaw goes on speaking while pointing absently to the tent and pacing the area. "Make sure you get shots of the entire scene so the CSI unit can work as quickly as possible. We want the coroner to get the autopsies started later this morning so we can recreate all this by the evening. Did you see the photographs he left behind?"

Frank turns away and stares up at the clouds churning across the dismal sky. From the look on his face, I don't think he finds much comfort there. He mumbles, "I don't know if I've ever seen a case as gruesome as this. Well, except for one..."

Harshaw whirls and brings his gaze to bear on Frank, fists tightly balled at his waist. "Better get a grip."

Frank lunges quickly toward Harshaw, stopping inches from his face. "That's somebody's little girl. Someone's son. I had a daughter that age..." As he trails off, I think Frank will leave it at that, but he regains his composure and presses on. "I don't give a shit about your accomplishments at the academy. You could be an investigative genius. But I haven't seen you do a damn thing except pace circles around this scene. So don't you dare judge me."

Harshaw's collar barely hides the flush crawling up his neck. "Look, I didn't mean any—"

"Then keep your cocky attitude to yourself. You've never had to notify parents, or wives, or husbands, or worse, been notified yourself. I've had to go to over a hundred doors of next of kin and it never gets any easier to give news like that."

That's Frank. He doesn't put up with anyone's shit. This agent could be the director of the FBI and Frank would still give him a piece of his mind.

A few silent seconds go by that feel like minutes. Harshaw clears his throat deliberately and looks to Frank for assurance that he can continue on with the case at hand. Frank stands proud and nods, having taken charge of the scene.

"I've seen these elements individually a number of times. But it's interesting that the killer has added so many personal components. We've got the photographs, the message, the posing of the victims, and the sheer amount of time he appears to have spent with them, it's surprising. This could be the beginning of something terribly lengthy if we don't solve it soon."

As I step back from the bodies, I can see photos scattered beneath the chairs and littering the ground around them. Thin white frames containing square images within them. The photos are covered in droplets of blood, smeared and runny from the rain. Some of the photographs captured the couple smiling, kissing, and having a good time. There are other photos that show what looks like an argument between them. The killer had been watching them for a long time. He's controlled and extremely patient.

"With all the noise from the heavy rains we've been having, he could have been quite close to the victims and they wouldn't have heard the camera," I say, "Instant cameras aren't as loud as they used to be."

A photograph only captures a moment of a person's life. It doesn't reveal any of what happens before or after the shutter closes. Maybe that's why people like taking photos. It's a way of capturing a split second of happiness. For all we know, the rest of their life could be miserable.

On each of the photos, "LIES" is written out on the message area in red permanent marker. Only one photo is free of comment. It sits in the center of the collection, surrounded by a wreath of lies. The one in the middle was taken postmortem, it's the scene the killer staged for us, his victims propped up in their camp chairs.

Maybe a photograph can capture truth only in death. I went into forensic photography because it would give me the opportunity to capture the one moment in a person's life that will never change. Besides taking my mind off my own horror-filled past. Thinking about that has me on edge. It's the beginning of September, but this line of thinking is giving me chills. I remember nights in one of my foster homes where I was locked out in the garage and forced to sleep on an old twin mattress that was infested with bed bugs. It was late fall, and the garage wasn't heated. Depending on how upset I'd made the foster parents, they'd leave the garage door open to make it even colder. All I was given was a thin sheet. I learned the hard way early in life that it was better to keep my mouth shut than to end up out in the cold.

"It won't take me very long to capture the entire scene. I think the photos are a way of telling us that he only saw truth in their death."

Frank was talking to the local PD and interviewing the hiker who found the bodies. He and Harshaw look over at me simultaneously after I speak. I can feel their eyes on me now, but I won't take my eyes off of the victims, off these photographs. I escape into my viewfinder. My camera always feels like protection from the rest of the world.

Looking through the viewfinder, zooming in and out on the photographs, I add softly, "I mean that's just my opinion. I'm just here to shoot the scene and leave the deductions to the detectives and agents."

Frank surprises me by speaking first, "No it's not that, Lydia. It's just interesting that you picked up on that so quickly. Looking at the scene, it makes sense, especially with that last photo placed so carefully in the center."

"Frank's right," adds Harshaw. "I'm glad that we've got you on this case. You'll be able to give us an inside look at the photographer's point of view."

I walk around the entire campsite, taking photos of everything. I come to the edge of the campground and gaze out across Norton Lake. The rain has subsided, and for the moment, things are calm. Near the edge of my vision, pine trees hover above the lake's mirrored surface, thick with fog.

A few paces north of the site, I come to a small waterfall. I close my eyes and listen to it. The sound brings me back to a camping trip, the only one I've ever been on. It was with one of the revolving sets of foster parents. I remember them arguing all the way to the campground, but I can't remember what the fight was about. When we arrived, my foster dad grabbed his fishing gear out of the truck and stomped off to find the river. Later that evening they made up, and wanted to pose for a photograph. She strapped the camera onto a tripod and set the self-timer. We all grinned at the camera and waited for the flash. With our arms around one another, and holding marshmallows on sticks, we crouched around the fire. From that image, no one would have guessed that the previous few hours had been hell for all three of us.

I realized then that a photograph can certainly take you back in time. Far beyond a moment frozen in bytes or in celluloid, a photo can capture much more than just what's in the frame. There can be all these unpleasant memories surrounding the one positive one that you were aiming for.

I snap myself back out of the memory. I have work to do, and I have too many reasons to be excited for this case. This killer took his time with these victims. He feels the need to explain why he chose to murder these two and wanted them to be found. Would there be more victims? He could have killed before. Maybe we haven't found the bodies yet. But if this is his first time, what finally drove him to enact his dark fantasy? I need to know more, and I know that tonight I'm going to fall asleep staring at a collage of photographs, a circle of lies surrounding the truth.

Chapter 3

ADAM

I've always enjoyed the wilderness. There's nothing better: camping in the parks and forests, hiking on back trails, or scrabbling up peaks. I live to be in the mountains, by the rivers, or on the lakes. It's the only time I can ever truly feel like myself. It's a home of nature's wondrous creation.

Which is why, standing in line at the outdoor goods store, I am becoming increasingly irritated with this woman. This twit is whining to her boyfriend and making her negative, small-minded opinion very clear to everyone in line.

"I don't see the point of this crap..." she says, wearing skin-tight workout clothes that match her running shoes, with a little backpack slung behind her. It's one of those garbage promo things, made of nylon and string. She's on the short and petite side, with bronze hair falling to the right, past her shoulders. At least the layers of makeup plastered on her face will make great bug protection.

Her boyfriend's been staring straight ahead this whole time, not even flinching at her incessant whining. Silence fell between them at one point when he didn't encourage her. It was great. But now they're back at it and hugging. She's taking a photo of them with all their newly acquired gear. If I were this guy, I'd take her on a hike and then push her made-up face off the side of a mountain to watch her tumble down, hitting every rock on the way.

It was clearly a lie. They're right here in front of everybody living a lie. She shares one fake photograph across social media, and it just eats me up. Only a few minutes ago, she was practically begging him to call off the trip, and now this fraction of a moment, snapped by her phone, would be what the world saw. They're tourists, that much is obvious. They're both wearing shirts sporting the names of universities. They probably float along, living on daddy's money, or by racking up student loans. It's pretty odd that they have to buy this hiking gear. Is this a last-minute trip?

I'm tired of keeping this bitterness inside. Why should other people live out their happy little lies when I can't meet someone to be myself with? I'll walk by a couple screaming at each other on the street, and think that at least they're showing their true colors. When I was younger, I embraced my darker side. I took joy in terrorizing other people. I've never killed anyone, but I've thought about it plenty. I don't think I can stand meeting yet another lying couple, another fake person, or another family putting on a façade. It's all too much. I may not be able to make her understand me but I'm ready to finally do something to make myself feel better about all the liars.

I gave Lauren so many chances, but she never accepted me. It's been months since our bitter end, but it feels like only yesterday. I had shed the outer layer of myself and opened up to her. I let her get too close and it drove her away. We had a brief relationship, but with plenty of passion and tumult.

One night, in bed, I released a part of myself, I let it take over. I held her down and slowly slid my right hand from her shoulder to her neck. At first, it just rested there, but after a time I could feel my grip tightening, fingers pressing into her delicate flesh. I blacked out and woke up to the sound of a scream. I must have let go because she was instantly on the floor and looking up at me in terror. She said that my eyes had been so empty. I was on top of her, looking right at her, but I was absent. She said I looked like a fucking monster. She rushed around my room in her bra and underwear frantically grabbing her clothes and shoving them into her purse as she fled.

At the time I didn't consciously mean it, but I think it ignited a part of me that had been dormant for years. There was such satisfaction in it. I can only imagine how good it will feel when I don't have to stop and I have the power to take the last breath from someone.

We didn't speak for weeks, but eventually, after she had had a chance to lick her wounds, she arranged to meet me for coffee. I arrived first and watched her approach the restaurant from my alcove across the street. I wasn't about to wait at a table by myself and look like a fool if she didn't show up. She approached cautiously, looking around the cafe, and took the table by the door. I knew that wasn't by accident. She wanted a quick escape. She slipped off her coat and laid it over her chair. She was about to take off her scarf but hesitated. It strikes me as nostalgic and a little hypocritical that she would decide to wrap her poor little neck in that scarf, the same scarf that I had used to tie her up. When things were still good between us, she had asked for it—a little bondage, a blindfold—and I would take my time to make her moan.

I remember walking across the street and into the cafe, not taking my eyes off of hers. She fidgeted in her seat as I sat down.

"Thanks for coming," she said, looking down at the tablecloth and fumbling with empty sugar wrappers. She jumped a little as I reached across the table for another sugar packet to mix into my coffee.

"I was surprised to hear from you. I was hoping that maybe you under—" She cut me off with a gesture before I could finish my thought.

"Maybe I do and that's the problem." I could tell she was starting to regret coming out here. "Maybe I don't and you're just a sick fuck that I'm lucky to be done with."

Her voice started to rise, but she restrained it before it caught the attention of any other diners.

"I thought you understood me, I hoped you did. I was only starting to show you who I really am. You can't handle it."

"You're right. I can't handle it, I can't handle nearly being strangled to death. And I can't handle having my boyfriend gape at me like a zombie, like I'm a piece of meat. I don't even think you were looking at me. You were looking through me. I was just, just... I don't know."

"Why did you want to meet me then?"

"I wanted to tell you in person to stay away from me. I don't want any confusion, I don't want anything to do with this new sick and twisted side of you. I didn't think you believed me a few weeks ago."

"I believed you, that's why I haven't gotten in contact."

"Maybe not, but I've seen you watching me. It makes me uncomfortable, you need to stop" Lauren says, gripping her napkin fiercely.

"Deep down you like it. You may not want me back, but you do enjoy the attention you always have. Why else would you wear that scarf?"

Her face flushed bright red, and she stood so quickly that her chair tumbled over onto the ground.

"I know I don't want any more close encounters with you. I don't want you near my body or my heart ever again. I really hope you do find the fucked up woman of your nightmares." With that, she left the cafe with the same fervor that she left my bedroom with only a few weeks earlier.

I didn't keep any photographs from my relationship with Lauren, they'd just show fleeting moments of happiness, they couldn't show the whole story. Maybe if she had accepted me, I wouldn't need to release my rage onto all those who lie to themselves and to each other. I wish I'd been able to get sufficiently close to her to share myself. I need to share the lies I suffered from my family and the abuse I survived at the hands of my mother. I need to find peace with myself, even if that means I have to do something violent. I know if I ever do find someone who embraces my dark side completely, they'll have to trust me unconditionally and accept my dark impulses. This person may not even exist, so for now, I should have some fun. Maybe I'll start with this "happy couple."

Chapter 4

ADAM

I can't believe I haven't tried this before. After a few minutes in line, I decide that they would be my first. Since I couldn't stand the dippy whiny girlfriend, she'll get to watch as I kill her hiker-wannabe boyfriend.

They make their way back to the streets of Portland and I follow them, hardly bothering to keep any distance between us. I listen in on their conversation for some key points. His name is Eric; hers is Kasey. After a few blocks, they step into McDowell's Books to browse hiking guides. I work at McDowell's a few days a week, more for the store discount and the people-watching than for the paycheck.

They make their way to the travel section and I approach them, talking to Eric like I would if I was on shift. "The travel section can be really overwhelming, especially our collection of local guides. Are you looking for a specific hike or camping area?" Kasey stands beside him looking just as bored and irritated as she did in the outdoor goods store. Eric looks up gratefully as he says, "Well, we were thinking of going to the Gorge to camp but with as many tourists as we see in the city, I can only imagine how crowded it would be there over the next few days. Do you know any places that are a little more secluded?"

"I know some spots that are so secluded they may not even be in those travel books." I wait patiently to see if they will take my bait.

"Yeah, that would be great, thank you. How'd you get one over on these guides?" Eric raises the three travel guides held in his hand.

"I never liked camping near other people, it just takes the enjoyment out of it, so a few years back I found a half dozen or so remote camping spots throughout Oregon. And I know exactly which one I'll lead you to. It won't be highlighted in those books." It will be so quiet this time of year. Good for them. Ideal for me. "If you're willing to drive out of the city there's this campsite a few hours south. It's very remote. It's off of a reservoir and it's free. Should be deserted this time of year. Maybe a few locals, but definitely no tourists."

This shouldn't be so simple, but here I am leading them right where I want them to go.

"We do have a rental car, and if this site is free, we could even stay for a few nights."

Kasey's eyes are glued to her phone. Eric looks at her and then back to me and gives a quick sigh.

"There's a place down there to rent canoes, and the fishing is lively this time of year," I say, grabbing a scrap of paper. "I can write out directions for you if you're interested. This spot will really give you an unforgettable Oregon camping experience."

The man looks hopeful about this opportunity to get out of the city. Even if he doesn't have the guts to break things off with this girl, I'm more sympathetic to him than I should be. I'm still infuriated by them. Between his weakness and her ignorance, they're useless.

A few minutes later, I write him out the directions and casually ask when he'd be going down there. He says there was no time to waste and that they'd be heading down there straight from McDowell's after a quick stop at their hotel.

People give out information so casually. I'm so thankful that the charm of this city lets the tourists open up so quickly. In a couple of short minutes, I find out that both he and the girl are from the Midwest—Ohio in particular. They just graduated from the University of Ohio and they're taking a few weeks off before starting their careers. Both of their families are on respective summer getaways in exotic places like Hawaii or Jamaica. Meaning there won't be anyone to check up on these two over the course of the next few days, these kids do so love their independence.

I wait outside, across the street from their hotel, and watch as a valet loads all of their hiking and camping gear and they check out. The girlfriend still looks unenthused. She's disgusting the way she clutches that cell phone to her face. She doesn't appreciate the man she's with or the unforgettable experience he's trying to create for her. She makes her way to the passenger side of the rental car in her stupor, only looking up once to give him a peck of a kiss. She doesn't meet his eyes for longer than a second before she drops her gaze, consumed by her phone once again.

I pull off of I-5. We're getting close. I've been following them for about two hours. They made one stop on the way, and so did I. My heart is practically beating out of my chest now, and I can't stop fantasizing about finally having a moment of complete control and release. This is what I've hoped for, waited for.

There needs to be some kind of justice for people who lie and deceive one another.

As they make their way to the Upper Lane Creek Campground, I pull past and park a bit farther down Mill Pond Road. I carry my kayak down to the water and slip into the boat.

I went home quickly while they took their time back at the hotel. Maybe before having a late checkout, they decided to have a quick fuck. I gathered what I knew I would need from a number of different stores in the area and a few things from home. My camera, film, markers, rubber gloves, rope, binoculars, some surprises, and, most importantly, one of my uncle's switchblades, were selected especially for this occasion.

The forest is dense around Upper Lane Creek, so I know I won't be seen as they set up camp for the night. I make my way quietly across the river and stow the kayak under some branches on the creek's bank. I find a V-shaped tree close to their campsite, and wait a while, resting my head on my pack. Through the lenses of the binoculars, it's clear that no one else is here. It starts to rain while I watch. A little while on and the drizzle turns into a downpour. I can see that Eric got the tent set up and was able to build a fire under the awning before the rain began in earnest.

It didn't take long until Kasey started complaining again. She's blaming Eric for taking her so far out into the woods and forgetting to check the weather. I quickly put my binoculars away and pull the instant camera out of my bag. With the rain, they certainly can't hear the click of the shutter. I can't use the flash, so I know they'll be captured as silhouettes, soaked and isolated. Whoever finds these photographs may not be able to see their expressions, their rage. What a shame.

"If this trip is your way of trying to save our relationship, it's not going to work. I'm done," Kasey snaps at Eric.

"I knew we were having trouble," Eric offers, "but I didn't think it was that bad. Why would you even come if this was how you felt?" He starts to pace. "Deep down I hoped I would feel differently. Maybe we could have a fresh start with this new transition and begin our new lives together. I think maybe we need to be apart, at least for a while."

Eric stares at her with heartbreak in his eyes. Without saying a word, he storms off towards the lake. As all of this is happening, I take photograph after photograph. They're going to kiss and make up in the next few minutes. I know that they will just lie to themselves rather than face hard truths. I want to be able to show them their hypocrisy, show them just how much they depend on their lies. There may be some love, but most of what the world sees is the result of the insecurities they've piled up around them. These two could never fathom being alone in this world. They're so codependent, it's sickening.

As predicted, Eric comes back to find Kasey sitting on a log by the fire, crying. She looks up at him with tears running down her face, guilt and hopelessness take over. He kneels down and pulls her into an embrace. They share some low whispers and come out of their embrace warming and cheering up by the fire. It's clear that they haven't really discussed the incredibly divisive issues eating away at their relationship.

Kasey pulls out her phone—surprise, surprise—and they plaster fake smiles on their faces. She just has to capture this beautiful moment of togetherness. This is the only photogenic moment of their trip. Thus far, they've hardly been pleasant to each other, never mind *happy and in love.*

I know it's almost time. As excited as I am at the sheer thrill of this, I want to leave something behind, a little puzzle with some purpose. The photographs show so many lies. The two of them can't be honest with themselves, even when they're fighting.

I drag my kayak into the water and hop in, paddling cautiously and quietly. It doesn't matter too much. The Oregon rain is on my side. Staring at my reflection in the water, I have a vision of my darker self frozen beneath the waters.

For many years it was as if this true version of me was looking up at the world from below, pounding against layers of ice, pleading to be set free. The whole time he was a spectator, forced to watch the meeker me tread the ice carefully and passively, always afraid of the misstep that would crack the boundary.

This other Adam is close. I can feel the warmth on his face as he nears the bright world above. That man below the ice has only surfaced once, briefly when I was a child and now it's time for him to resurface again. This time for good.

After making my way across I pull the kayak half on the shore and tie it to a nearby tree. I stare at them for a long time, we're only separated by twenty feet and a cluster of trees. Even though it's raining Eric is looking for wood to try and keep the fire going. Kasey is still sitting on a log in front of the dying fire basking in the sad harsh glow of her phone.

I move out from the brush and approach swiftly. Coming up behind her, I press the drugged rag tightly over her mouth and nose. Her struggles last for minutes, and my ears are focused on the steady rustling coming from the distance. Between the mild suffocation and the chloroform, she eventually submits, her muscles give out and her head lolls to the side.

My eyes darted around the campsite. I still can't see Eric, but I can hear the snap of branches now at the edge of their campsite. I have a little more time. I drag Kasey's rag doll body away from the light of the fire, gag her, and tie her to a nearby tree. As I'm tying her up, she fades in and out of consciousness, so I press the rag against her nose and soon she's knocked back out.

My heart is beating so hard that it is difficult to hear Eric as he treads the rain-soaked ground. I close my eyes, stand as still as a statue, and listen as his footfalls grow louder. My eyes shoot open, and I grab his shoulders from behind, throwing him headfirst into the tree. Slumped on the ground in a mess of branches and blood he tries, slowly, to get up. I throw my bulk on top of him, driving his arms down into the wet mud with my knees and I wrap the chloroform-drenched rag around his head. He's already on his way to passing out from the blow to his head, the drug only helps the process go quicker. He hardly thrashes before he's lying there limp in mud up to his cheek.

I drag Eric to a tree across from where I've stashed Kasey and I secure him to it. After the gag is tied, a faint murmur comes from Kasey's direction. I'm excited that she's waking up. Now things can begin.

Her eyes open slowly, and there is only a moment before she starts to panic. Her wide eyes search all around and land on Eric. A flush comes to her cheeks and her eyes moisten as she begins to realize the terrible situation she's in.

I stand above her, and she squints her eyes. It must be hard to make out my face in the black of night. The fire is dying behind me and she's still very groggy. I can see the recognition coming on. She recoils like I've struck her as she recognizes the person standing over her and realizes that I won't be letting her live. I wear no mask and make no attempt to hide my identity. I stand proud and ready.

I drop my backpack onto the ground and take the knife out of my back pocket. I'm wearing rain gear, gloves, and a hat. I open the knife carefully and feel the blade between my fingers remembering my uncle and his obsession with these knives. He'd probably roll over in his grave if he knew that *I* was using them for this torture. I grip the handle and walk over to Kasey. Her eyes aren't straying from mine. Her body thrashes violently as I get close. She opens her mouth to scream but all that comes out is a pathetic muffled cry through the gag.

I run the edge of my blade from her temple to her chin, tracing the path forged through the makeup by her hot tears. The knife dances lightly there but I don't draw blood yet. I move the knife side to side across her chest, down an arm, and then along the back of one hand. She changes tactics now, utterly calm and still, paralyzed with fear of the blade. It could break her skin at any moment.

A few minutes later, Eric awakens and repeats the groggy dance of recognition. He wears not terror, but defiance on his face. I watch with amusement as he attempts to wiggle free but gives up quickly as he feels the strength of his bonds. There is little point in struggling.

Now that they are both awake, the real fun can begin. Starting with Kasey, I take the tip of the knife and stick it into her stomach. It pierces the skin drawing a slow red trickle down her white tank top, the stain growing in uneven concentric circles of red, creating a tie-dye look centered on the wound. I move the knife tactfully from side to side to make the wound wider and put pressure on the handle until I've lost an inch of knife in her belly. Her head shudders and shoulders sob as the knife lingers deep inside her. On her sweaty, damp face there is only pain. Her eyes start to roll up, and I yank out the blade to shock her back to the present moment.

Her bleary eyes shoot open and race back and forth between the man she superficially loves and the man who's going to end her life. I stand up and watch the blood pool in the folds of her clothing. I have time since it will take quite a while for her to bleed out. So I reach into my bag for the photographs and toss a few at her feet so she can see all the lies she's been living. "They're all lies." I spit the words at her and point to the photos. "You can post your precious memories to social media and reminisce, thinking fondly of the way things were, but you're just lying to yourself and to each other." I walk over to Eric and toss a few more photographs on the ground. I decided that since he seemed to be honest some of the time, she could watch him die and not the other way around. I stab him slowly, forcing the switchblade deep into his chest so that the only part of the knife still visible is the grip. I pull the knife out, wrenching it clockwise as I adjust my hold and repeat. With every stab I can hear Kasey's muffled wails. After only a few moments Eric's head collapses, drooping between his shoulders. I kneel down to examine his eyes. They're empty of life, but I can still see in them the emotions he was experiencing as his wounds accumulated and the blood left his body.

When I turn back to Kasey, she starts to struggle again. As if she has any chance of surviving what's to come. I stand up, not taking my eyes off of her, and slowly wipe each side of my blade on Eric's pants.

When I walk over to her the sobbing ramps up, it wracks her shoulders. Each convulsion brings a flash of pain to her face. She's visibly shaking and anxiously shifting in place. Her legs, her fingers, and her jaw are twitching and clenching. The frantic motion moves through every part of her body as it fights for escape. I straddle her so I can get a better hold of her neck. Even through my gloved hands, it's intimate. I feel truly dominant with her life held firmly in my grasp. Her death isn't on my hands. She got herself into this situation. She lived a lie and exaggerated the shreds of happiness that she and Eric shared. Instead of working on their relationship, she spent her time sharing photos and embellishing memories for *likes*. She seduced others into believing she and Eric were perfect and happy to create jealousy among the people who cared about her the most.

Kasey looks bewildered as I take off her gag. She's frightened by the uncertainty. But it's no mystery. I want to hear her gasping as she takes her final breath. I bring my hands together around her throat, pressing my fingertips against my knuckles until my hands shake uncontrollably. I release my grip and stare into her eyes. They're rusty with burst blood vessels. I stab her over and over until she finally stops fighting.

I don't know how long I've been sitting here on the bare ground, but in front of these corpses, I've experienced more peace and clarity than I've had my entire life. Of course, I know they'll be discovered, but I don't care. In fact, I hope they're found soon. I'll reposition the bodies to send a message and leave all the photographs behind. Part of me revels in thinking about it, the detectives standing around and trying to decipher my message. I'm sending a clear one, no need to be mysterious or vague. There's not a trace of evidence to tie me to this, and I've no discernible motive for killing these two. I can't wait to watch the investigation unfold, sure they'll stumble down their blind alleys and make feeble attempts to draw leads out of the meager information they have.

I'm not sure if I'm going to kill again. It's difficult to imagine pushing this feeling aside, leaving behind something that gives me so much satisfaction. Only time will tell.

Chapter 5

LYDIA

It's been a few days since I first toured the crime scene at Upper Lane Campground. During that time, I've been called to the station daily to give my opinion on one or another piece of evidence and to comment on the killer's photographs.

My obsession has shifted. The portrait of the little girl that once hung on my ceiling has been replaced by reproductions of the photos, surrounded by enlarged prints of my photographs from the scene. I've taken down more than just the one photo. I virtually redecorated my apartment with Upper Lane Creek photos. The night that I got home from the crime scene, I practically stripped the walls, pulling down all of the photos in my apartment and replacing them with ones the killer had taken. A photo of the couple's cold, lifeless hands hangs in my bedroom. Their fingers are intertwined, and at the edge of the frame, ligature marks are visible along the wrists like bracelets of thorns. Another photo hangs beside it, showing their volatile fight. A dozen such photos of the couple line my ceiling in chronological order, giving me a glimpse into the last evening this couple shared. These snapshots and more adorn my walls and vie for my attention. Staring at them, I wonder about my place in all this.

Frank and Agent Harshaw are letting me be very closely involved with this case. Under these circumstances, it's encouraging and frightening to know that my opinion is considered so valuable. But I need to keep my guard up around them, so as not to come off like a killer myself. I can't admit how much I actually think like him.

I sit on the floor crossed-legged with the case files surrounding me and scan the coroner's report. According to forensics, the male victim, Eric, was killed first. Both Eric and Kasey had been gagged and they were bound to two adjacent trees, facing one another through their torture and eventually their deaths. The preliminary report says that the killer had drawn things out for quite a while before the murders were effected. Postmortem, he untied them and positioned them like dolls in their camping chairs. He manipulated their heads, arms, fingers, and even posture to take the final photograph.

Upon removal of the clothing, forensics notes that both bodies have ligature marks on the wrists and ankles. Taking into account body temperature and stomach contents, along with rigor and livor mortis, time of death lies somewhere between 8:00 p.m. and 9:30 p.m.

Besides the multiple stab wounds and incisions inflicted on the torso, both victims also have multiple wounds in the upper extremities consistent with defensive injuries. It's fascinating to me that the killer displayed so much rage, especially when killing the female victim. The pathologist reported that there were many overlapping stab wounds making a definitive count difficult but in general at least 30 unique punctures were found on her torso and arms along with another 20 defensive wounds in evidence.

Even when they're not asking me to go down to the station, I try to find a reason to get involved. I want to know as much about this case as possible. In past cases, I haven't shown this much of an interest. Once I leave a scene, I usually leave my camera's memory card with CSI, the unit can then log the forensic photos as evidence and assign the proper metadata to each image. I rarely make much effort to retain my photos. The exception is murder cases, especially this one. I've handed off my primary memory card to be logged in the case file like usual, but my DSLR allows for the data to be saved on two cards simultaneously. Essentially this offers me two distinct copies of all photos—one on an official card to be submitted and logged, and a second redundant card that I can keep.

I've told agent Harshaw that I want to become familiar with the different stages of a multi-agency homicide investigation. Since I'm already assigned to this case, in my capacity as forensic photographer, this would be the perfect opportunity. He's agreed and has allowed me to sit in on a number of briefings, including one that's about to start.

Frank sits next to me in the meeting. His nerves are building as the days pass and the case stagnates. We're without any official leads and I think that Frank's afraid this killer will commit another murder, this time in his jurisdiction. At that point, the pressure would definitely be on Frank, as roles changed and Agent Harshaw became the second in command. Worse still, the difficulty in keeping a major investigation quiet would increase if our next crime took place in Multnomah County.

There are only a few people privy to this conference call with the FBI profiler in Quantico. After the conference call, Agent Harshaw will be briefing the team and I'll be allowed to stay for that too. I'm excited. I know two people are dead, but this suspect has me intrigued. I've read about so many killers and it's exhilarating to be this close to someone so complex. So often these individuals are misunderstood. The FBI profiler hasn't given our team his assessment yet, but I don't think the perpetrator is killing for fun. I think this is something he believes he has to do, like it's his calling. I think he's just beginning to project his true self and to act accordingly. Maybe he's tired of pretending to be a mild-mannered person.

The profiler dials in, and Harshaw switches the receiver to speaker.

"Agent Jonathan Yates here. I won't waste any time, and I'd appreciate it if you held questions to the end. I'll begin.

"It is clear that these murders were intimate. The killer chooses to put his hands on the victims and he violates them with copious knife wounds. Those who choose to kill with a blade or other type of close-contact weapon tend to be playing out some strong emotion. Some vendetta or passion that they need to express.

"This one was definitely careful. Taking a lot of time with the victims but leaving no trace of evidence. The scene didn't contain one fiber, hair, fingerprint, or drop of fluid not originating with the victims. The film is of a type commonly bought online and available at many brick-and-mortar camera stores. The writing on the photos, the word 'LIES,' was interesting and led me to believe that this killer has been traumatized by lies in his life."

While listening to this dry profile, it's difficult to ignore my surroundings. We're in a room too small for the number of officers involved. Our exodus will look like a clown car once the meeting is over and we file out of here. There are six chairs around the table and fifteen PPB asses to fill them, so most of us stand. The different tiers of bureaucracy are well represented in the room. This case is definitely getting a lot of attention from within the department and without. No one here is particularly fresh, as most of the department has been working hard on the collection and interpretation of evidence since the initial find in Norton. I can smell day-old cigarettes on rumpled suits and from the smoke-stained fingers of these men. I can see yellow sullied armpits in white cotton shirts, and stale sweat permeates the room since there's only one window in here and it's locked firmly.

"Somewhere in this person's past, a very significant lie changed the course and view of his entire life," Yates says. "He may have had other victims, but we can't be sure. The urge to kill has certainly been troubling him for ages. Maybe some other crime or release was satisfactory in the past, but the aggression and frustration have peaked recently. There's intelligence and patience in this crime. Finally, it's difficult to say anything about his physical appearance."

Agent Yates speaks to the group with a formal tone, but he hesitates throughout the brief summary. The majority of the points in his profile are from textbooks I read years ago. And these criminal profiling techniques are no more complicated than the ones we discuss in my courses on forensics.

Harshaw jumps in, announcing himself. "This is Harshaw, Yates. We agree with all of that on our end. Now, he stabbed the victims while they were down on the ground with their backs against trees, so it's very difficult to be specific about his height. And I definitely think he's familiar with the outdoors, especially this campground in particular. But it's the victims I can't place. Why were they there?"

"Why do you say that?" Frank says. His eyes are fixed to the speakerphone and he's wearing a far-off expression of contemplation.

"Well, the killer knew exactly where to watch them from without being seen. His footprints led straight to the water, which makes me think he had a canoe or kayak since there were no tire tracks other than from the victims' rental car. He must have parked his car somewhere relatively close to the crime scene," Harshaw declares, rather sure of himself.

"Upper Lane Campground is very remote, but it isn't abandoned," Frank says. "The lands around Norton Lake get almost eight thousand visitors a year."

"Sure, but not only is this site remote. It's free. It's a perfect draw, but how many tourists have you ever seen this far out of Portland camping around Norton?" Harshaw looks at me. I'm pretty sure his question is rhetorical, but I try to be a good guest and answer, "None?"

"Right!" He begins to smile. "Tourists go to Mt. Hood National Park or the Gorge area. But this spot is ideal for a couple looking to get away and avoid the tourist experience. So the question is: How did they find it?"

Harshaw stands up so abruptly that his folding chair snaps shut and totters before it crashes to the ground. His eyes dart around the room and he's lost in thought, Harshaw smiles as he focuses on Frank, and smiles like he has the answer to his own question.

"He talked to them. They didn't come here on their own. I think they were led here by the killer. How else would they have found the campground?"

Frank looks up at Harshaw, and for the first time during this investigation, they're in agreement.

"Yates, do you think this matches your profile?" I can hear the anticipation in Frank's voice.

"That would definitely fit in with my profile," Yates continues. "He's manipulative and charismatic. Your classic sociopath. From the photographs he's left us at the scene, we know he spends a lot of time with his victims and he had a definite purpose in the two murders. He spent a lot of time with the victims both in preparing for the attack, hidden away in the forest. And then he took more time still when they were bound and gagged, leading up to the murderous act. The heightened danger and risk of discovery was certainly not a problem he concerned himself with. It's very difficult to tell how long he had been planning this. Regardless he seemed to know when to strike these two. If it was last minute he was very careful. He remained in control and delayed the pleasurable release. He had built up considerable anger and hatred toward these two individuals. There were no signs of sexual assault with the victims, so we know that wasn't his motivation. In front of you is the full profile, but those are my highlights."

I leave the station clutching the case file to my chest like a stack of school books. I've got Yates' report, the full criminal profile, and between that and the various case notes, I have plenty to study. The Portland Police Bureau isn't far from one of my favorite spots downtown, McDowell's Books. It gets busy, but there's something incredibly soothing about being surrounded by people, all reading, engaged in different subjects. I make my way into their café, find an empty corner seat so there's no one behind me, order a mocha, and put on my headphones. As instrumental music begins to pump through my headphones, I start reading.

File No. 98-6745-163

Date Received: 9/8/23

From: Dr. Jonathan Yates

Federal Bureau of Investigation (FBI)
National Center for the Analysis of Violent Crimes (NCAVC)

Behavioral Analysis Unit (BAU)

935 Pennsylvania Avenue, NW

Washington D.C. 20535

Quantico, VA

The bodies of a man and woman were discovered at 7:00 a.m. at the Upper Lake Campground in Horton, Oregon. Both were stabbed multiple times in the abdomen, neck, and arms. The killer left behind Polaroids with the word "LIES" written into the memo section in red permanent marker. All photos, except one, contained the message. These Polaroids consisted of photographs of the victims at the campground. The one Polaroid, intentionally left blank, was the only photograph in evidence that was taken of the couple postmortem.

PROFILING INPUTS

The items used in the double homicide were limited to those brought by the offender. No blade or tool was found at the scene that could account for the wounds sustained by the victims. Therefore it appears that the offender did plan the crime; he would have brought a knife, rope, chloroform, rags, and duct tape. It is also possible that upon leaving the scene the offender took possession of any such objects as were used in the capture or murder of the victims. The only objects left at the scene were several pieces of cloth, tests confirm residue from chloroform to be present on these rags. The crime scene indicates a highly premeditated event, the killer stalked or waited for his victims. The offender may have even encountered the victims earlier in the day. The crime scene is the same as the death scene in this case.

Investigation into the background of the victims revealed that the 22-year-old, 125 pound, 5'3″ white female and 23-year-old, 180 pound, 5'8″ white male checked out of a hotel in the Portland area around 12:30 p.m. The victims had visited a sporting goods store shortly before checkout, sometime in the late morning, approximately 11:00 a.m. They purchased a variety of expensive hiking and camping equipment. All items purchased were in evidence at the scene. No theft is evident.

The medical examiner's report indicates the cause of death of both victims was loss of blood from multiple sharp force stab wounds. Evidence of sexual assault is absent, no semen was found on the female victim,

additionally, victim was lacking contusions or trauma on the inner thigh. Although no traditional sexual molestation is evident, the specific attention paid to the female victim indicates that the offense may have been sexually motivated.

The preliminary police report reveals that a day hiker, a white male aged 29, discovered the victims' bodies. The hiker did not have cell service and drove to the local police station and reported the homicide. Police at the scene were unable to locate any witnesses who had seen the victims after they checked out from their hotel.

DECISION PROCESS

The crime scene describes a double homicide. The offender's primary intent was to kill, making this a violent crime with motive unknown. There was a degree of preparation indicated by the level of sophistication and organization at the crime scene. The idea of murder may have occupied the thoughts of the offender for an extended period of time.

Victim risk assessment reveals that the victims

are self-sufficient. Both of them were capable of traveling to an area far from home. Individually the female victim would not have posed a significant threat to the assailant; her small stature means she would be fairly easily overcome. There is no evidence to indicate that she struggled successfully against her attacker, such as flesh beneath the fingernails. The male victim is of a more threatening size and physique. His stature is average, but his weight and physical tone make him a more imposing opponent. His wounds were consistent with a surprise attack, leaving no opportunity for retaliation. Due to the presence of two victims it would have taken considerable tact and skill to coordinate their separation from one another. Separating the victims was necessary in order for the assailant to maximize his advantages of surprise and possibly greater strength. The offender was able to overcome the two victims through patient observation and committed action at a pivotal moment. There is limited information available on the two victims; we have two moderate-risk adults due to their lack of familiarity with the area. This area has not reported any similar crimes. The victims were at higher risk because of the extreme remoteness of the crime scene. The likelihood that they would discover such a remote site on their own is low. They may have been introduced to the area by the offender.

The crime is considered moderate risk for the offender due to the likelihood of his being discovered. As well, the offender likely put himself at great risk by

conversing with the victims at another location and in broad daylight. The time commitment for the crime is worth noting; the amount of time the assailant spent with both victims greatly increased his risk of being discovered or of leaving behind evidence. All of the activities with the victims—photographing, binding, gagging, and the use of a slow agent like chloroform— would have taken a substantial amount of time.

The location of the crime suggests that the murderer felt at ease in the area and was quite familiar with it. The crime scene indicates that the assailant felt quite confident that he would not be interrupted.

CRIME ASSESSMENT

The double murder was one event rather than a series of events. The victims were probably incapacitated in rapid succession and the murders most likely occurred within minutes of each other based on the decomposition of the bodies. It appears that this may be a first-time killing. The offender is an atypical organized killer. There were elements of both organization and disorganization, therefore the offender falls into a mixed category.

A reconstruction of the crime/death scene renders a general image of the crime. To begin with, the victims were not necessarily stalked for a long period, but

were chosen by the assailant for reasons that are presently unclear. There are no indications that the offender had intimate knowledge of the victims, nor personal motive. The victims were unimportant in and of themselves, but the subject needed to kill them in order to carry out his violent fantasies. This is not likely to be a crime of opportunity due to the remote location. The assailant can be assumed to be familiar with the area and may have lured the victims to the crime scene in order to ensure a low risk environment in which to pursue his fantasy.

The killer controlled the victims through the use of superior size in the case of the female victim, and blunt force trauma in the case of the male victim. Throughout the sequence of events, chloroform was used multiple times to maintain the incapacitated state of the victims while he bound and gagged them. The female victim was dragged, not carried, to the campfire. This could indicate that the assailant is of small stature, or that he took great care in preventing trace evidence, such as hair or fiber, from being transferred on to the victim. Overlapping marks and residue from duct tape, on both victims, indicates that the assailant removed the tape and reapplied it at least once. The offender stabbed the male victim to death; this was followed by the female victim's strangulation and eventual stabbing. The female victim received significantly more stab wounds than the male victim, and was the only victim to show ligature marks. The assailant took his time at

the crime scene and was extremely confident that he would not be interrupted. The murderer displayed his control of and contempt for the victims, postmortem, positioning them in camping chairs propped against each other.

The crime scene dynamics suggest that the crime was opportunistic. Some aspects may have been part of a persistent fantasy for the killer. A calculated plan of torture and murder could be set in motion once the offender had victims. There is also an element of imagery with the staging of the victims' postmortem and of the scattering of the photos on the ground at the victims' feet.

CRIMINAL PROFILE

Based on the information gathered during the previous stages of this report, a criminal profile of the offender has been established. A physical description of the suspect states that he would be a white male, between the ages of 22 and 35 due to the general age of the victims. He would be of average appearance. He would be of high intelligence, and is probably a college graduate. He may be unemployed currently or in a career that offers him a high degree of independence.

Specific rage and hatred toward the female victim, was evident in the method of execution. This may indicate that the subject has difficulty maintaining close relationships with women. If he has had any type of relationship with women, he would primarily associate with younger women, due to his need to dominate and control. The crime scene reflected, in the postmortem treatment of the victims, that the assailant felt justified in his actions and that he felt no remorse for the murders. He was not subtle, leaving the victims positioned in the way he wanted them to be found which indicates the subject may kill again.

INVESTIGATION

There has been a media blackout associated with this crime due to its gruesome nature and the remote location, and because the victims were tourists.
A day hiker came upon the camp site, and notified police at the local station. They in turn notified Portland Police Bureau and the forensic crime scene unit. The FBI, county district attorney's office, and the medical examiner's office were all simultaneously notified. A task force was immediately created of

approximately 18 detectives and supervisors as well as 4 agents.

If the profiler believes that this killer doesn't fit the pattern of any other open cases, especially serial murder cases, then it really may be the start of multiple murders. There's no pattern established except for his focus on lies. So many people are guilty of lying, no one is safe. Not even me.

Especially not me.

Chapter 6

ADAM

The sun is out, which is rare for Portland, but not unheard of despite the reputation our city gets. But this weather, at the end of summer and the beginning of fall, is definitely exceptional. It's attracting all sorts of people to our fine collection of natural tourist traps. It's mostly day hikers that live in the city, but this time of year, tourists start to trickle into the Willamette Valley from all over the world to experience the Pacific Northwest.

I stumbled onto my first set of victims by accident, but now I crave another. It's important not to choose someone who is from Portland, someone who would be expected home for an early evening meal. It's nauseating to have to picture it. The worried wife or the concerned husband sitting at the dining room table staring at the clock. After dark, they call the police reporting that their significant other was only supposed to be gone for a day hike. Tourists generally don't watch the news after a day of traveling or sightseeing, so they aren't going to be concerned with some local news about a murder or some disappearances.

I just stumbled upon that first couple, but everything worked out so perfectly. They were whiny assholes, they were from out of town, and they were begging to be led away from the city. It was way too tempting and too easy. No one is even going to be looking for those two for days. If—well, *when*—I decide to kill again, I think it's crucial to find another couple, or a family, on vacation just to make things easier. Most of these tourists have their travel guides with them. That way, they can visit whichever local breakfast place is listed as part of "the essential Portland experience." I generally choose a Saturday or Sunday to venture to one of these restaurants.

I arrive early, before the rush, and open one of my favorite books, *The Silence of the Lambs*. Thomas Harris' writing possesses such eloquence. He really understands the dual nature of murder. He's able to describe a man who can be brutal and full of murderous rage, but without robbing his character of the calm, insightful, and refined characteristics that make Lecter so very dangerous.

I drink my third cup of coffee as I eat my plate of eggs, smothered in cheese, and a side of thick-cut bacon. I'm listening to the conversations as they unfold around me. I close my eyes to focus on the intoxicating aroma of the freshly ground Arabica beans. The conversations fade into the background, then all I can hear is the faint echoing chorus of the woods on a damp night. I'm taken back three weeks, to the night I had my very first kill. I shut my eyes so I can recall the horror and the shame on the girl's face as I thrust my knife into her. The satisfaction of gutting her could only be second to the thrill of sliding my fingers around her neck, nearly choking the life out of her.

I'm taken out of my daydream by a nearby conversation. I can hear a family talking about how much they're enjoying their Portland vacation.

They're sitting in the booth behind me, but I can see the woman's reflection in the restaurant window. She's eyeing her husband while their two children go on and on about how much fun they had yesterday at the Museum of Science. I begin to imagine how I would do it, how I would kill them. But I'm not a monster. I realize why I've never killed before and why I was finally able to in Norton. I was presented with victims who were suffering. Their lives were overburdened by the weight of their deception.

Now, I know what you're thinking. Aren't I guilty of living a double life? Aren't I dragging down the mean decency of our society by quietly plaguing this corner booth of mine? Sure I am, but I've finally decided to do my part and rid the world of at least a few cretins who deceive the people that they're supposed to love the most.

The family members all have chestnut hair and olive eyes. They're overflowing with excitement about the coming days, about getting out of the city to explore what the Pacific Northwest has to offer. They're unable to contain it and I can't blame them. Oregon boasts a variety of colorful ecosystems. We have ocean, mountains, and desert, all within a few hours' drive of each other. Oregon has the ability to make you feel like you're in a completely different country without ever leaving the state.

After a few minutes, I gather that they are going to drive somewhere at least a few hours away for some tent camping. The family seems nice enough and I can tell that the husband adores the wife. He's been keeping constant, gentle, contact with her. Whether it's playing with a few strands of her hair or running his hands idly on her arms and down her back. She seems distant though, always looking out the window. Her mouth wears a smile, but not her eyes, and she keeps one hand, cautiously, at the edge of the booth. That hand keeps caressing her purse and I can see the outline of her cell phone in the outer pocket. She's probably feeling for the vibration of some incoming text.

This is just another family living a lie. It's so rare for a person to know everything about their partner, or their parents. Our most shameful secrets and our innermost thoughts hardly ever come to light, even in the best relationships. But if you can't share who you truly are, that deception will be the wedge that drives you apart. This family may appear happy on the outside, but the husband and kids know nothing about the wife's affair.

On my way to the bathroom, I can hear her on the phone by the doors. She's facing the corner and trying to be discreet, but she couldn't fool anyone. The way she's carrying on, with her flirty smirk and low slutty whisper, it's a wonder the husband doesn't catch on. But people are way too willing to let the status quo remain, leaving the truth unspoken. They stand there watching as their lives grow tiresome and moldy. We have these powers of observation, and we can see the writing on the wall, but we never make that pivotal move to change things. That's not me. Not anymore.

"I miss you too..." she says. "Well, I didn't think we'd be here this long either... It's just a trip. It doesn't change anything between us, I promise... I don't know if I'll be able to call again, but let's meet at our usual spot next week. I love you so much."

Her smile at the table had nothing on the one that slid across her face when she took that call. She's so fake, the bitch. But who knows, maybe he's cheating on her too. Back at my booth, I'll collect more information on these people. My next victims.

I can't be sure if they were going to go camping on this trip, but I know I'll have to put the idea in their heads if I want to control where they end up. A brilliant idea comes to mind, and I can't help but smile.

I pick up my cell phone and casually mime dialing a number, then wait on an imaginary second party to answer on the other end. I speak loud enough for them to overhear me. "Really? That's awful news... A landslide in the Multnomah Falls area? I was going to head up there this afternoon to camp for the night." A lie. "No... I don't mind driving farther out. I really wanted somewhere that wasn't going to be crowded anyway." Actually, quite true. "Oh, I've never heard of that, it sounds beautiful though. Thanks again."

The family man behind me leans over my shoulder and says, "Excuse me, sir. I didn't mean to eavesdrop, but were you talking about the Multnomah Falls area?"

It's so easy to reel them in. I hope they have enough time to go farther out to a place more secluded.

"Yes, I was. They were hoping to open up some camping areas today but apparently there was a landslide. Now it's looking like it's going to be closed for at least a couple more weeks." I pile on the convincing story and watch the father and kids heave a sigh of disappointment.

"Oh, that's terrible news! We were going to head up there this afternoon and camp for a few days. We're not from here. Visiting from New England. I'm being rude. I should introduce myself and my family. I'm Andy. Andy Baker. This is my wife Claire and our two boys Sam and Nathan."

My heart starts to race as I know I'm only a few short hours away from my next slaughtering.

"Well, I was just talking to a friend of mine who works for the parks service. You don't want to camp in the Multnomah Falls area, anyway, not at this time of year. If I were you, I'd drive a bit farther out and find somewhere more secluded. Some place where you won't run into a ton of tourists." If they bite onto this, I'll be able to take my time and catch up with them after sundown.

"We do have a rental car, but we only researched a couple places to camp, spots that were in our guidebooks." Andy gives me a guilty smile and holds up some travel books. He steals a sweet glance at his wife and then looks back to me, hanging on for a response. He doesn't even know that minutes earlier she was running her whore mouth to her lover back east. I think about how close I am to leading them to their death and it gives me such a rush.

"I know of one place that's about three hours south of the city. It's right on the outskirts of the Willamette National Forest. There're endless trees covered in moss and by one of the campsites you can hear running water from a small creek."

"That sounds perfect. How much is it?" Andy asks. "Are there hiking trails nearby?"

Claire starts in before Andy can continue. "Hon', that would be a long drive for the kids. I really think we should just head home early. I mean, I'm not sure it's worth it to go even farther out of the city if we can't camp where we planned to."

She's probably thinking that she'd rather not wait a few more days to get good and fucked after being stuck on this family trip so long. Her husband and children clearly aren't a priority to her. That makes this even easier for me.

"Sure, but we were going to go for a few days, and this sounds so much more secluded." I can tell that Andy is contemplating it as Claire anxiously awaits his response. She looks at him with such eagerness, pleading silently for him to drop the idea. For an instant, I imagine what those eyes will show me later tonight—the piteous stare that she'll offer in exchange for her life and for the lives of her family.

"Well, we're probably only going to get out here once," says Andy, still mulling it over. "I think we should make the most of it."

I chime in to make sure I can push him over the edge. "To answer your question, there's a trailhead right across the parking lot from the campsite. The name of the place is Mineral Falls Campground in Cottage Hill Grove. It's right off of I-80 and it's such a tranquil place. I'll never forget the trip I took there with my family when I was a boy."

"Thank you so much. We're so happy we ran into you. I don't know where we would have ended up if we hadn't."

We exchange smiles all around and they begin to study their maps with a new purpose. As I turn around in my booth, I can see their reflection again. I see them start to plan what will be the last night of their lives.

Chapter 7

ADAM

They believed me so easily. There was never a family trip. I can't even decipher who was who in my family. My mother was very young when I was born. While she was still pregnant, my grandparents shipped her off to live with my aunt and uncle in Astoria.

My first memories should be of my mother or my father, and, at the time, I really thought that woman *was* my mother, but she was my aunt. They had me believing that I was their son and that my mother—my *real* mother—was her sister. My life growing up was built on a lie and full of deceit. I'll never belong anywhere, never be able to trust anyone. My origin has been eroded. It was stolen from me.

It was the truth that did the most harm. I could probably have gone on living the lies if they had never told me the truth. I hated my aunt and uncle for shattering the memories I did have. Everything was tainted after I found out. How could my mother have agreed to this, how could she hope to give me anything nearing normalcy? How could the people closest to me lie with such ease and so frequently? From that moment on I would resent liars, especially people who lied to their family. To those closest to them.

My uncle was a drunk who gave out beatings every time he got the chance. He collected switchblades, keeping them in an antique glass case. On occasion, he would walk over to his glass case and slowly open the door. His eyes were ablaze whenever he came at me, but his movements were always serene, slow, and full of menace. He would inspect his blades, his hand hovering first over one, then another, before he would select just the right one to terrorize us with.

I think I was around six or seven when I realized I could play too. One day, the drunken shit was passed out on the living room floor. I walked carefully over to the knife case. Without taking my eyes off of him, I slid the cabinet door all the way open. I took each switchblade out of the cabinet and arranged them in front of me on the carpet. These types of blades usually have a safety lock system to keep the blade from releasing unless you depress a certain spring or contact. I held up a four-inch, pearl-handled stiletto and fingered the catch to release the blade.

I relocated his knives across the room, a few at a time, until I had a cache right by my uncle's head. His snoring was obnoxious. He was on his stomach and splayed out. Now, I'm disgusted at the thought of him, but back then, I was angry. I wanted to see him hurt. So, I took each switchblade and flicked them open. I moved slowly and purposefully placing the knives around him, fanning them out. They formed a cordon. The knife points were just centimeters from his flesh. The last one I placed directly in front of his sleeping eyes. And then I waited. I was delighted as I sat on the couch, watching him for signs of movement. There were twenty-five switchblades surrounding him, and I hoped at least one would penetrate the skin.

I sat there on the couch with my legs crossed under me, it was almost two hours before he woke up. He saw the blade in front of his eyes and started to thrash. Four blades ended up breaking skin and a good amount of blood seeped into the den carpet. It was so satisfying.

That's where it started for me. How can one ever hope to have a normal family or adult relationships after growing up surrounded by lies, abuse, and fear?

"Can I get you anything else?" says the waitress, who sports a little black ring in her nose and tattoos all down her arms. She aims an impatient look above my head.

"I'd love another coffee," I fire back cheerily with an award-winning grin. Her shoulders relax and a smile spreads slowly across her face.

"I'll be right back with that," she says.

This happens everywhere I go. Some people are so easy to manipulate. Like Andy over there, he trusted me as soon as we started chatting. I'm charismatic, articulate, and confident.

I check on the family behind me. They're still in their booth, smiling and laughing, about to pay their check. The man turns around in the booth as they get up to leave.

"Well, we've decided to head down to Cottage Hill Grove this afternoon," he tells me.

"You really won't regret it. It'll be a trip you'll remember for the rest of your life. Are you at a hotel nearby?" I ask.

"We got a great rate at the Economo Lodge downtown. We just need to head back to pick up our rental car," he says proudly.

"It's always nice to save a little money and I'm sure you did well with the rental car too. They have such great deals now on SUVs. We haven't driven ours far yet, but we really like it, it's a red one. Since there are so many owned by locals, we thought we'd want a color that was easier to spot."

"Hey, what a good idea," I say.

"Well, it was great meeting you. Thanks again for the suggestion. We're so excited that we get to camp at a local favorite. I wasn't looking forward to going somewhere overrun by tourists."

"It really was my pleasure."

Sam and Nathan bounce up and down as they squeeze out of the booth. Claire looks annoyed and disinterested. Andy offers his hand to her, she takes it, and he plants a soft kiss on her lips. They interlace their fingers and smile at each other, and with their two children, they walk out of the restaurant without a care in the world. All but Claire. I'm sure she's dreading spending even more time with her family. Now she'll have to wait to see her pathetic lover.

The waitress brings me my coffee. It's still early, only eleven in the morning. I don't need to head after them until dinner time. I'll drive the three hours just to see if they've taken my bait. On the way, I can stop in some middling town and buy another beater truck from a mechanic. They always have some barely drivable piece of crap. As long as I pay a little above what's fair he won't ask questions. That should do the job of taking me to the campsite, and I can dump it after. I'm already anticipating the wave of intense pleasure associated with the kill, but will it bring me the same bliss this time? I think of the family laughing, hiking, making dinner, and setting up their tent for the night. If everything falls into place, this afternoon will be their last.

Chapter 8

ADAM

It's early evening when I hear their tires crunch on the gravel of the Mineral Falls Campground. It's difficult to hear their chatter over the sound of the creek and from this distance. I'm concealed on the far side of the campground behind the trunk of a tree. There's going to be just enough light for them to set up camp and make a fire. I was a little worried earlier when they hadn't shown up, but we are three hours from Portland and they have two kids in tow. I've been here for a few hours taking in the beauty of the moss-covered trees and the winding icy creek. I found a black panel van to buy from a local mechanic in a nearby town who would take cash. I have everything I'll need for tonight in the back along with my inflatable kayak, which has come in handy since I can't park too close to the campground. I revel in the seclusion that this site offers. Earlier, the sun moved across the sky. The moss on the trees shone a golden brown, backlit by the sunbeams. This place is spellbinding. It's fitting.

Sam and Nathan fling their doors open and spill out of the car as soon as it's rolled to a stop. Andy is visibly proud that his children are this excited to spend this time in nature and camp out for a few days. Claire lingers in their car, the small light of her cell phone shows pale on her face. The second Andy is out of sight, her bitter smile softens into a sultry smirk. It's clear who she's talking to, and it doesn't pain me at all to know that she'll never see this man again.

I study them through my binoculars, wishing the instant camera had any kind of range so I could capture moments of the evening as they unfold. The boys are roasting marshmallows over the fire and using the sticks as swords. Andy joins in for one of these duels, and his son stabs him through the heart. He makes a very convincing dead man. Their mother stays by the fire, looking deep into the golden flames. Now and again, she stares far off into the distance, almost straight into my camera.

Once it's dark, I slowly make my way across the creek. I know this campsite well, but there's only one place where it's safe to cross the creek. If I get it wrong, I'll fall in, and that could ruin everything. I'm wearing waterproof boots, but there is a section where I need to walk across some sunken driftwood. My pack is heavy. I have everything I'll need to make this night worthwhile for the whole family. I'm almost across when I feel a stick beneath me give way. Grabbing a branch overhead I threw all my weight at the muddy shore of the creek and lay still, in case they heard the crack. A few minutes go by before I stick my head above the creek bank to inspect the scene.

I had taken my time to think about the order because I wanted it to hurt Claire the most. The two boys are slumbering in their sleeping bags by the fire. Andy is trying to muster a little romance by the fire with his wife. She isn't having it though and instead starts an argument, waking the boys. They do have two tents set up, but the boys had pleaded with their father, tugging at the arms of his jacket, to let them sleep under the stars. He had agreed, but now the boys are sent into their tent so mom and dad can talk.

Before he can turn back to Claire, she's already storming off toward the car. It's so obvious. She had probably been struggling to think of a reason to go to the car so she could text her lover. It doesn't even take him a minute to run after her. Maybe he doesn't know? Maybe he does know, but he's afraid that if he says anything their pathetic attempt at family life would be destroyed.

I walk fast but quietly toward the tent. I need to drug the children first before their parents return but I have no idea how much longer they'll be. My heart is pounding rapidly, making it hard to think as I approach them. It's not anxiety or nervousness that plagues my heart's rhythm. It's the anticipation of my success that excites me, as I imagine stealing away their last breath. Soon I will put my hand on *her* chest and feel the heartbeat as it slows, and smile as it resounds with a final wretched beat. With the fire roaring away, it's a challenge to see out into the woods. If Andy catches even a glimpse of my face, I'll be done for. I approach the tent and run my gloved fingers over the front flap to get their attention and arouse their curiosity. One of the boys unzips the tent just enough to stick his head out and investigate the noise. Before his eyes land on me I grab him by the shirt with one hand. With the other hand, I bury his face in the drugged cloth and wrap my arm around him to pin his arms to the side. While I'm waiting for the first boy to go limp, the other one starts to scream. He only gets out a quick squeak before

I can grab hold of a pillow to muffle him under the combined weight of his brother and me. It takes a few minutes for the chloroform to take effect, which feels like an eternity. It's difficult to keep the second boy in place with only one arm while he's thrashing under the pillow. I let off the pillow and grabbed him by the hair, slamming his head against the ground once, hard enough to knock him out. After I make sure they're both sufficiently dosed, I move them both back into their sleeping bags for now.

I move behind a tree so I can get cover while I wait for their parents to return. It's only a few minutes before Andy trudges back into camp. He makes it easy and sits down on a log facing the fire, with his back to the tent, and to me. I'm surprised that he didn't go to check on his boys when he came back. He must not think that there are any madmen loose in these woods. That's just it though—I'm not a madman. I'll sit here and wait to make my move and joke about madness, but there is purpose in what I'm doing. He will wake up from the drug and I will strip the lies away from his life, and it will set him free. The truth will set them all free. I make sure the rag is soaked through as I creep up behind him.

I step away from the pit and drop the unconscious Andy several feet from the fire. While my eyes readjust to the darkness, I stand perfectly still trying to map my surroundings by sound alone. I have to find Claire as quickly as possible. As my eyes adjust to the darkness, I can see her face glowing in the distance. She is drawing me to her with the very object of her treachery. She holds her cell phone in her left hand, and it shines like a beacon as she twirls strands of hair with her right. She has all of the windows up in their rental car, even though it's so warm tonight. Except for this precaution, she's being careless. She's absorbed in her conversation and fails to notice as I walk slowly out of the trees and stand a few feet in front of her. Three victims lie in the camp awaiting their fate while the fourth sits right in front of me, oblivious to what is coming.

Claire is the picture of a harlot. She melts into her seat like a teenage girl with a crush, languidly flirting and hanging onto every word this guy says. It doesn't seem to bother her that she could be caught by her husband at any moment. I walk around the car assessing her escape routes and planning how I should approach her. I want her to flee to the campsite, so I need to approach from behind as she gets out of the car. I saunter around the rear of the car and sit and wait. It's irritating to have to wait and hear this garbage, but I need her to hang up the phone on her own. I can't have her lover questioning the last words he'd ever hear her speak. If I cut them short and end the call he'll be alarmed. If I force her to end the call her tone of voice will give it away, they could even have a safe word. Most couples with safe words only have one for the bedroom, but it's entirely possible that they could have one for a situation like this. So, I wait for them to finish.

I lean against a sturdy tree and gaze up at the night sky. The stars are obscured by branches, their great leafy mass swaying in the wind. I concentrate on their rustling, the cacophony of the forest at night is the most soothing music I've ever heard.

While I wait for the faithless wife to finish up her last phone call, I think of Lauren. One of the best memories that I have of her is from our first morning together at my place. I had never trusted anyone enough to let them into my life. I was coming back to bed, and she was sitting up, wrapped in the blankets. She looked so free and innocent. It turned me on so much that I had to have her again right then. We laid there together, naked, talking about our sexual pasts, both of us being cautious about how much we would share. I told her that if we continued dating—if that's what we were doing—that we should have a safe word. She blushed and laughed, then quickly got up and made her way to the kitchen. I thought maybe I had shared too much, but as I was lying on my back, looking at the ceiling, I saw something flying through the air. I caught it just before it hit me. I sat up abruptly and started laughing. She peeked her head into my bedroom from the hall, laughing, and yelled "Pomegranate!" Since then, any time we went out in public together, one of us would always use the word or subtly work it into conversation.

I stand here now in the wild darkness and my smile slowly fades. Even though she could never accept me, I still miss her, or at least I miss the idea of her. I know it's incredibly unlikely that I would ever find someone to share my life with. At least I'm finally being true to myself.

I hear the car door open, and I lunge forward before she has a chance to shut it. I'm clutching a fist-sized rock in my hand, and as I come upon her I slam it into her skull. I lift her arm and let it drop to make sure she's at least temporarily knocked out. I have to get her back to the campsite as soon as possible.

First, I take the SIM card out of her phone and crush it, then I break the phone against a tree. I shut the passenger door of the car, grab her by the hair, and drag her through the forest. On the path, I take her limp body over rocks and sticks. Her clothes catch on a few. Once we arrive at what is left of the fire, I tie her hands behind her back and her feet together. Claire looks dead already.

It doesn't take long to set the scene. I build the fire back up, and it crackles as I take the boys out of the tent one at a time. They're fading in and out, so I drug them again. It would be a shame if they woke up and spoiled the scene before it was ready. Then I place a dry rag in each of their mouths and cover it with tape. I wanted some variety, so, instead of using rope this time, I have zip ties to keep their arms and legs in place. It's easier to drag them around with them trapped inside of their sleeping bags. I start to drag Andy but have to stop after a moment. I can hear him faintly over the hissing of the fire. Andy is starting to wake up and moving around in his sleeping bag. I land a kick on the back of his head, just hard enough to keep him pliable. It would be a shame for him to miss the show, where would be the fun in that? Minus Claire, the whole family is arranged in their bags around the fire, making three sides of a square.

I make sure Andy and his boys' heads are sticking out of their sleeping bags. A groan rumbles from my periphery and I glance over at the mother. I cut the zip tie off her feet and prop her against the log nearest to the fire so she can see her whole family. Earlier, they had all squeezed onto that log to roast hot dogs. It's incredible how much a few hours can change everything. Think about that the next time you take something or someone for granted.

Claire starts to scream, as best she can through the gag. There's still a slight chance that someone could be driving on the nearby road, but it's unlikely. Even if they were, they'd be flying by at highway speeds this time of night.

I tower over her, smiling, and shake my head slowly and deliberately. Kneeling down, I grab a clump of hair at the base of her skull and cover her mouth with my other hand. I make sure to press all of my weight onto her. My eyes don't waver from hers.

"Now, Claire, there's no getting out of this, but if you want to say goodbye to your family, I'll allow it. You will not scream. You will not try to get away or hurt me in any way. If you break any of my rules, I will make this a lot worse for all of you. Nod your head if you understand."

This is a demand, not a question.

She nods her head at me, looking reluctant, like a dog being told to stay put. She looks around and sees her two boys and their father trapped in sleeping bags. One by one they stir and attempt to struggle against their bonds.

"Look at them," I say. "Look them all in the eyes and tell them what you've been doing. Tell them that your wholesome family life has been a lie."

As soon as I rip the tape off, the lying starts.

"What are you talking about?" she asks. So, she's going to play dumb. I thought she would recognize the severity of the situation without any further prompting, but apparently not. I pull out my switchblade and hold it up to her son's neck.

I rip off Nathan's gag and he cries out, "Mom please tell the truth. Don't lie. You're always saying lying is bad. Just tell the truth and say you're sorry." I tape the cloth back over his mouth. His eyes are overflowing with tears. He mumbles, still pleading with her.

"I think it's about time you stopped playing dumb and own up to all the lies you've told to the three people you're supposed to love the most," I say. "I saw you there in the car and hiding in a corner of the restaurant earlier today."

She looks from me to Nathan and Sam, and then locks eyes with Andy.

"I've been cheating on you," she says.

Tears well up in his eyes and he whips his head away from us. His shoulders start trembling in small waves.

"We haven't been close in a long time, but I just couldn't break up our family," she adds. It's a sad attempt at an excuse for lying to them every day.

His face reddens and he glares at me, jutting his chin out. I know what he wants. I remove the gag and let him talk to his wife one last time.

"I knew. Of course I knew, but it makes it so much more real now that you're finally going to admit to it. You're only doing it now because he has a knife to our son's neck. You make me sick. Ten years and two incredible boys and you'd throw that all away? You just can't keep your goddamn legs closed."

"I needed some excitement! Everything was so predictable, and I couldn't handle the monotony of our boring little life."

"Well, you got it. Isn't it exhilarating?"

"You think this is my fault?!"

I cut in. "Of course it is. I was drawn to you. To your deception. Your pathetic excuses won't get you anywhere with me. You're dead already. You know that much, right?"

They turn to observe me, like I'm intruding on a personal moment. Then they look at each other with something that resembles shock as the magnitude of the situation sinks in. They're tied up around a fire in the middle of the woods. There's no help out here, and they've seen my face. There's nowhere for them to run and there's nothing she can say now to get them out of this.

I tape her mouth up and move to gag Andy again so I can get on with the evening's festivities. He dodges his head out of the way and looks at his wife.

"You fucking cunt. I hope you burn in hell for this." The poison in his gaze remains as he turns back to me.

From the incredulous expression on her face, it's evident he's never spoken to her with such disrespect in their entire relationship.

I give him a pat on the head as I reapply his gag. I don't think I've ever had more respect for him than I do right now. He should be happy. At least he's going to die knowing he got to say what he wanted. The truth finally came out.

Chapter 9

LYDIA

I'm glad they're gone. My "family" I mean—not these four victims lying around the fire. At first glance, it seems like they're just some campers sleeping out in the open. The hiker who found them was on his way to photograph some wildlife in the morning light, and he thought he had come upon a fairly normal scene. It only took him a second to realize his mistake and call the police.

There's something about this crime scene that reminds me of my foster family. I was so happy to be rid of them. Of course, for Heather, it was terrible. She had lost her parents. But she was too young to really understand what monsters they were. After the accident, I ended up in a group home since I was fourteen and it's much more difficult for social workers to place a teenager. Heather was still young, and she was placed with a family eventually. Her case worker tried hard to find a way to repair her life, like that's possible after you lose your parents.

My track record was misleading to prospective foster parents. I bounced around from home to home, and nobody wants a kid that unstable. It was never my fault, but in the end, fear led me to a shithole group home. At least the abuse was over. No more late-night visits. No more cowering at the sound of footsteps in the hall. Even now, fear shoots through me when I see a light come on outside my room.

I was on a strict schedule at the group home, but we were given the opportunity to take up a hobby. I think they wanted to encourage us to have an interest so we'd be less likely to get into trouble. I guess I should count myself lucky that I didn't end up on the streets, addicted to drugs, or with a criminal record.

I channeled all of my emotions into photography instead. I remember the day the group home staff talked to us about different hobbies and interests. They didn't have a huge budget, but one option was an old instant camera. I received a little allowance every week from the state and I'd buy film. A few years later, after I had aged out of the group home, I found a used digital camera in a thrift store. I went back every week to make sure it was still there. Finally, after two months, I saved up enough money to buy it. It was only thirty dollars, but I was making next to nothing working in service. I was so proud the day I walked out of the store with that camera.

I left Seattle and moved to Portland with my savings plus a little bit of money the state had given me. I couldn't completely move away from the Pacific Northwest, but Oregon would be the fresh start I needed. I responded to an ad for an apartment put out by three people who were looking for a fourth roommate. It was in Old Town, and I went to check out what would be my first apartment in Portland. The people sleeping in tents and drug users on the street didn't faze me. I had seen a lot growing up in twisted, psychotic foster homes. The apartment was cheap, and I thought that if I could find a job quickly I might be able to afford my own place within the year.

It took some time, but I got started as a server in a bistro downtown, and I found another part-time job doing some administrative work. I was hidden away in a cube working for a soul-sucking company, but the pay was enough that I could save up.

I came to Portland because I needed a fresh start, and I guess Heather had the same idea. We hadn't seen each other for years. She had sent me a letter, a year back, saying she'd be moving to Portland and that she hoped I'd want to connect with her. In a way, I was relieved that I would have someone in the city, but another part of me was strongly hesitant. She would be an unwelcome reminder of my past. I had left it all behind and tried hard to forget that family. But that also meant I had abandoned her.

I saw her during closing time at the bistro while I was cleaning tables and flipping chairs. She looked about twice her real age, having withered into a greasy husk of herself. Her dirty hair was matted to her face, and she was dressed in clothes so filthy and shabby that the original color was unrecognizable. Through the window, I saw her digging in the garbage. She plucked out some colorful wrapper wad and ate its contents. I tried to think back to the last time we had spoken. She didn't know that I had been hiding the painful truth from her. I thought maybe it was for the best that I didn't have anything to do with her.

I started to walk away from the table that I was cleaning. I didn't really believe it could be her, but I had to know. With a pang of guilt, I turned around and headed outside to see the woman before she moved on. She turned to me, her brown eyes looked empty, but eventually, I saw a glimmer of recognition on her face.

"Lydia? Is that really you or am I hallucinating again?"

This was a genuine question, which broke my resolve, she seemed so disoriented.

"Yeah, it's me. I was hoping it wasn't you. When did you get here? What happened to you?"

"I don't really remember. The days kind of blend together," she said with a slight smirk. "I think I've been here about six months? I met someone and we really hit it off. He's a bouncer, so we partied a lot. We lived down in the Pearl district for a bit, but he kicked me out when I started showing."

Once she moved out from behind the trash can, I could see the swollen belly under her rags, as well as the track marks on her arms. My face caught fire and I started sweating even in the December weather. I was furious that she was shooting up while she was pregnant. I couldn't bear the thought of her child growing up in the system.

I found out later that she didn't have a drug of choice. She once told me that as long as it was free or cheap, she'd snort, shoot, or smoke anything that was put in front of her.

She named her son Jacob and was quickly deemed by the state unfit to raise him.

I offered to help her get back on her feet. She went through rehab and got clean, and she earned back custody of Jacob. They moved away from Portland to Northern California so that she could stay out of trouble. That was seven years ago.

I can't believe I've lived in Portland for over seven years. Heather and I used to keep in touch every few months, but it's been almost a year since her last call. A few weeks ago, she sent a letter out of the blue, saying she wanted to come up with Jacob for a visit. I've always been nervous about her visiting, but it's been a long time since that cold December night when she was living on the street.

I don't talk to her much, but I hear from Jacob almost every week. Our relationship is the closest I've ever had with anyone. After Heather went to rehab, I fought hard to gain temporary custody of Jacob. The court granted it since Heather's parents were dead and I was the closest thing they could find to a family member. For the year it took her to get clean and work her way through rehab, Jacob and I were inseparable. That was the only time in my life that I ever felt normal. I sometimes catch myself reliving those memories. I took so many photographs of us around the city. Now I'll go to those places where I used to take Jacob and I'll sit, eyes closed, and listen to the sounds. Then I'll open my eyes and look at the photograph of us in that particular place. We went to the carnival, took rides on the tram, went to McDowell's, the library, and took countless hiking and camping trips in the Columbia Gorge. I'm sure he doesn't remember that year like I do since he was so young. I remember it though, and that's all that matters.

Since it was the first year of his life, I got to experience many of his firsts, building an even stronger connection between us. It became easy to let people believe that he was my son. Heather had told me before she went into rehab that she didn't want to see either of us while she was there. She wanted me to take one photograph of Jacob on the first of every month to send to her as motivation. I agreed and really did hope, for Jacob's sake, that she could get clean and stay clean. I knew deep down that I couldn't be a mother to him in the long term. I was too fucked up to take care of anyone.

Despite being so close with Jacob, I've never had the courage to have him back for a visit. Maybe it's finally time to have them over to see if I can salvage some version of family life. Heather talks about how much she misses her parents, but she didn't know them. She doesn't realize that they would have eventually killed us. Back then, I had no choice. I remember the last time I saw that house. It was right before dawn, and the two of us stood in front of the burning house, my prison for the previous two years. It would have been her prison too if I hadn't done what I did. I saw freedom in the flames.

I bring myself back to the present, still standing in front of the slain couple and their two children. Why would this killer murder the entire family? There's definitely a pattern forming. Both crimes occurred in remote campgrounds far away from the city and both sets of victims were tourists. Photographs were found at this scene as well. Again, we have multiple images of the victims with all but one having the word "LIES" written on it, this time in blood. The CSI team is going to test the blood type to see which of the four victims the blood may belong to. Maybe that will give the team a better idea as to how he may be choosing the victims.

Frank has been on edge all week, but he does seem relieved that Agent Yates, the FBI profiler, is going to be joining us on-site tomorrow. Everyone involved with the case is calling this the beginning of a serial killer. Though no one has come up with a clever name for him yet.

Frank pulls up to the campground and walks over with some manila folders in one hand and a coffee in the other. He always looks irritated unless he's on to some lead for the case. And Agent Harshaw has become withdrawn and miserable since he failed to predict the killer's next move or even provide a victim type. I think he's giving himself too little credit. With the second murder involving a middle-aged married couple plus children and the first involving an unmarried couple in their early twenties, there was no way to predict who the next victim or victims would be. We assumed there would be further victims. The killer was driven. Part of me couldn't wait. I'm learning more about him with every shot I snap and during every meeting with Harshaw and Frank. Each night, I study his work. I've filled my apartment with the crime scene photos and his snapshots. Little by little, I'm getting to know him—perhaps even admire him.

Agent Harshaw lowers his phone and approaches the group. "I was just speaking with the cell carrier for the female victim, Mrs. Claire Baker. Been on for the past three hours and they were finally able to tell me about the last call from her device. She was talking to her boyfriend."

"Her boyfriend..." Frank replies. "I guess we know why he killed them."

"S'pose we do." Harshaw starts pacing around the campsite. "He watched them like he did the first victims. Maybe he tied the boys up first. They probably would have gone to bed before their parents."

Frank adds, "If she did make a call last night, she was probably away from the campsite, by the car, so that may have given him the time he needed to drug and tie up Mr. Andy Baker."

I listen to their theories while I take photographs of the scene. It doesn't really matter whether or not they figure out how he did it. It doesn't change the fact that he's taken the lives of six people and they have no idea when or where he will strike next. They go back and forth for a while, stroking each other's egos so that they can feel more in control of this unpredictable situation.

There are more photographs this time. I center one lying inches away from one of the boys' feet within my viewfinder. Since there are four victims, our killer has involved much more of the campground with this crime. Though some of the images were taken from a very far distance—as that was likely the killer's only way of concealing the mechanical noise—I can make out scenes of the family laughing and roasting hot dogs by the fire. In one photograph, the father is pictured looking dejected and fitful, sitting alone next to the fire while his boys were presumably in their tent for the night. Another photograph shows the wife on her cell phone, sitting in the car. Finally, we have a postmortem photo of the family, tied, gagged, and in their sleeping bags.

I can distinguish a bold line between the original forest green color of Andy Baker's sleeping bag, and the crimson stain that has welled up from deep within it. Only two of the victim's bags are blood-soaked. It appears that both of the boys died of strangulation and may have mercifully been unconscious during the ordeal. Even though our killer didn't stab the boys, he still felt the need to kill them. Maybe he saw that as a mercy. There's definitely tenderness in his treatment towards the children that he's lacking with adults. All four victims' heads are sticking out of the top of their sleeping bags, which are zipped with drawstrings pulled tight. Mrs. Baker is puffy and pale, her face appearing like it sustained some damage before death.

The medical examiner walks over to Mr. Baker and unzips the sleeping bag. He pulls back the top layer of insulated nylon, revealing multiple stab wounds in the victim's chest, neck, stomach, and upper arms. His ragged flesh lies beneath torn clothing, and shreds of stuffing litter the inside of the bag. His wounds are consistent with the defenseless posture of one trapped in a prone position. I'll know more tomorrow after the autopsies have been conducted for all four victims. It's difficult to say how many stab wounds the male victim has. A dozen maybe? But however many times the blade penetrated him, with the female victim that number was doubled. Her upper torso is grotesquely disfigured from the collection of wounds. There is hardly any unbroken flesh visible on her.

I make sure to capture every part of the campground before I go back to the parking lot. I take photographs of the car, but there don't appear to be any signs of forced entry. Backing away from the car, with my eye to my viewfinder, I stumble over a branch and nearly fall backward. When I'm distracted by my work like this, I can't see anything but my wide shot. I steady myself and look down to see a blood-stained rock lying on the ground. I realize that at some point during the night in question, *he* was standing here, right where I'm standing now. I take it in from every angle, trying to move through the scene so I can share it with him. He must have smashed this rock over her head so he could drag her back to the campsite.

Frank drives me back to the station in the late evening. We're both caught up in our own thoughts, so, mercifully, the cab is silent for the journey. All I wanted to do was stare at my viewfinder and go through the crime scene over and over again.

Chapter 10

LYDIA

Early the next morning, Frank and I sit beside each other on a bench in the station lobby. The day's briefing starts in a few minutes. I got us a couple of bitter coffees to drink while we're waiting. I can't think about anything other than our new victims, and I silently try to urge the day along. It's going to be hours before we can get the full rundown from the coroner and the forensics lab. And by that point, Agent Yates will have the momentum of the meeting wrapped up in his updated criminal profile. Yates flew in from Quantico last night and should be ready fairly soon. Frank is in a daze. I think he was really shaken by the discovery of the family this morning.

"You okay?" I ask, knocking my knee against his.

"I don't know, Lydia. This case..." Frank pauses and his eyes drop to his coffee. "I've never seen anything like it, and you think... You *hope* you never will, especially this close to retirement. I've got enough going on in my head, I don't need this case haunting me too."

"You can't let it get to you, Frank. You're gonna drive yourself mad."

"There's nothing else to it, I just can't stop thinking of my daughter. She'd fit in this case. Somebody like our offender could be responsible for her death too. We've got to get more on this guy. We have too many bodies and we've hardly built any case. This killer is so unpredictable. Sure, we've got a handle on motive, but that isn't going to do a damn thing to narrow down our pool of potential victims."

I know I can't say anything to help ease his worries, so I speak the truth. "You're right. Anyone could be next. And this guy is clever. We've got tons of physical evidence, but unless he screwed up, all the hair, fiber, and DNA samples are going to come back as belonging to the victims. Just like with the first scene."

"That's great. Lydia. Reassure me some more."

I care about Frank. He's like the father I always wanted. Sweet, devoted, a little gruff, and sarcastic to a fault. I hate to see him so down.

"If this is only his second set of murders," I muse, "he could have made a mistake."

"He could have, but I doubt it. Like you said, he's clever. He's been nothing but careful and controlled so far."

"Everyone has a breaking point. He's acting out fantasies that are extremely risky. He's bound to lose control. We just need to be ready when that happens."

"And we *will* be." Frank manages a faint smile.

Agent Johnathan Yates appears at the end of the hallway, walking in our direction with caffeine-fueled conviction.

Frank stands and tugs at my arm. "It's time."

We make our way into a windowless conference room, which looks exactly like the lecture hall I use for my Teacher's Assistant classes for the Forensics Department at Portland State. I sit down in the third row next to Frank and pull out my legal pad and a pen. I'm more excited today in this pseudo-classroom setting than I ever was when I attended college.

Agent Yates centers himself at the bottom of the conference room, peering up at the rest of the attendees as they shuffle into rows. He speaks before everyone is seated. "As some of you may have guessed, the FBI has now taken over jurisdiction of this case. With the results from the recent autopsies, along with the updated profile of the suspect, it is safe to say that we have an established pattern in both the method and preferred environment for the crime. We will, of course, keep all local law enforcement involved and work as a team so that we may pool resources.

"The Bureau is extremely thankful for the cooperation it has received thus far, and I personally applaud the careful discretion under which all have operated these past weeks. As we all know, this is a very sensitive case. Now, I believe we have some new data derived from the physical evidence." He points to the medical examiner in the second row. "If you wouldn't mind coming forward."

The medical examiner, having just sat down, waddles toward the steps and joins Yates at the base of the room. "I would ascribe the cause of death of both the female and male to be the multiple stab wounds in the chest and neck. Additional wounds sustained contributed to rapid exsanguination. The two boys died of strangulation. The blood found on the photograph is a positive match for the female victim, as well as the blood found on the rock by the victims' rental car. It is difficult to establish an exact time of death, but I was able to determine the order of deaths. The children were strangled first. There is no evidence that the two boys struggled, there were traces of chloroform in their systems. This indicates to me that the killer drugged the two victims before killing them. This was followed by the death of Mr. Andy Baker and finally Mrs. Claire Baker. In all victims' blood work, we found low concentrations of chloroform. No examples of foreign fingerprints, hair, or fiber were found on or around the bodies. All DNA samples tested match those belonging to the victims. On the rental car, we found the four victims' fingerprints as well as countless examples of foreign prints. These must be dismissed as extraneous, as the vehicle has been utilized or rented by dozens of individuals in the past few weeks.

"Those are the highlights, and you can find the complete report in your most recent briefing."

Everyone in the room glances through the report, and I wonder if any of them are as eager to learn of Agent Yates' revised profile of the killer as I am.

Chapter 11

LYDIA

I walk out of the briefing excited to go back to McDowell's to read the revised profile. I love McDowell's. There's something so intimate about going through the stacks and running my fingers along the spines of the books.

As I exit the building, my phone vibrates.

A call from Heather.

Then I remember. Heather is coming to town with Jacob. With the case, I completely forgot it was this week.

I answer. "Hello?" It's just a single word, but my voice is shaky and I hope she doesn't notice. I've talked to Jacob a handful of times over the past few years, but not Heather.

"You didn't forget we were coming in today, did you?" Heather says with a hint of snark. "I sent you some texts this morning. And yesterday.

And the day before."

I take the phone from my ear and scroll to find the unread messages. Sure enough, they appear in bold text. I completely missed them.

"I knew it was this week," I respond. "I'm just... really involved in a case right now."

"I thought you would have taken some time off to hang out with us."

"I would have liked to, but this new case, I—uh," I stammer. "I'm getting better access to the case files, and I'm involved in all the briefings. I've been asked to work on this case exclusively." It's not until I say it out loud that I realize how proud I am of my newfound status, though I know it means nothing to Heather and won't do anything to resolve her annoyance.

And I'm right. "Well, I'm glad you could squeeze us in," she says.

"It's not like that, Heather. This is a huge deal for me." I take a breath and gather myself. "You wanna go grab some food?"

This softens her up a bit.

"Let's go to the food trucks downtown," she says. "Jacob has been pretty picky lately. Maybe we can head to McDowell's after, just like we used to."

"Yes! Food trucks!" Jacob yells in the background, out of breath. It sounds like he's jumping up and down on a bed. He's always had ridiculous amounts of energy. "Hi, Aunt Lydia! I want tacos and books!"

"He's excited to see you. I mean, he's been begging me for weeks." She almost sounds bitter about it.

"I've missed him. And you." I don't miss her. I feel like I'm lying to her and to myself every time I think of her. That's why I never went to see her in California, and why she wasn't invited here either. "I can't believe how many years it's been," I add.

"It didn't have to be. We can talk more later. Does six work for you?"

"Yeah, that sounds good. It'll give me time to go home and freshen up." And take down all of my graphic photo collages, just in case they want to come by after dinner.

I arrive at the food trucks downtown, scanning the crowd for Heather and Jacob. I wonder if she'll look different and if I'll even be able to recognize Jacob.

But then I see him speed-walking down the sidewalk, with that same boyish face I remember but with his once-smaller body stretched from head-to-toe. His shaggy mop of brown hair bobs wildly as he darts toward me, along with some boxy object swaying from his pants pocket.

Heather follows behind him, clasping Jacob's hand as they weave between people. She doesn't realize he's spotted me yet, and appears annoyed that she's being dragged through the crowd. Jacob breaks free of her grip and runs straight for me.

I kneel down and put my arms out. I almost fall over onto the cement as all seventy pounds of him barrel into me.

"It's really you!" Jacob exclaims.

"Of course it's me, silly," I giggle, ruffling his hair.

He reaches into his pocket and grabs a bulky, white, rectangular object too big to be a phone. It presses it to his eye and I look into the open aperture of the lens.

"Smile!" he yells before snapping a picture with a loud *click*, which prompts a mechanical whirl. A photo exits through the bottom of the camera, color seeping its gray face.

Seeing the camera flips a switch in my brain that takes me back to the case—back to the murder scenes.

But Heather doesn't let me stay there for long.

"You can't just run off like that," she scolds, walking up behind him, grabbing his arm, and whipping his body around, causing him to drop the quickly developing photograph.

"I'm sorry," Jacob says. "I just wanted to see Aunt Lydia."

"An instant camera, huh?" I say to Heather. "Very retro."

She grunts. "He loves it. The pictures are so expensive, though. I limit him to two a day. He says... he wants to take pictures like his Aunt Lydia."

It doesn't bring her much joy to say this.

Jacob, apparently at his two-picture limit, stuffs the camera back in his pocket, then picks the photograph off the cement, which has turned into an embarrassingly silly candid photo of me looking down at him. He stuffs it in his other pocket.

There's an awkward moment of silence as Heather looks from Jacob to me, attempting to force the scornful mother look off her face. She gives me a limp hug and says, "You look good."

"So do you," I say into her ear, and I honestly mean it. While she'll never be able to wash away the years of drug abuse evident on her skin, she looks like the best possible version of herself.

"Shall we?" Heather says as she releases me.

We make our way to the food trucks. It doesn't take long for Jacob to create some distance between us.

"Stay within my sight, Jacob!" Heather barks. "Do you hear me?!"

"Yes, Mom," he calls back, getting farther away, but making an effort to look back and do as his mother says.

He's a good kid.

"So, how have you been?" I ask Heather. "How's California?"

"It's going. I'm working as a teacher's assistant at Jacob's school. It's only part-time but it pays the rent. He has a lot of friends and seems happy."

"Are *you*?"

"Am I what?"

"Happy."

"Oh," she sighs. "I haven't been happy in years."

Since her parents died.

I'm still not sure if Heather ever considered me family. We never got close during the two years I stayed with her parents. I wasn't allowed out of my room very much, only for meals and my homeschooling lessons. Heather got to go to public school, but not me. I've got to give them credit, though, because, of course, I would have talked about the abuse. I would have told anyone who would have listened.

"I'm a single mom that had to flee the state to stay sober," she continues. "I have a son that I've never quite connected with and a life that just doesn't feel like mine."

I don't know what I can say to her. I'm not sure if I could form a connection with a child if I were in her shoes. She was away for his first year of life, and that year of bonding can't be replaced.

"Books, books, books!" Jacob yells, spitting out the debris of hastily-eaten tacos as we walk toward the entrance of McDowell's. He runs through the door.

"Jacob!" Heather yells.

I rush after him through the maze that is McDowell's Books. The sheer size of this place surprises me every time I walk inside.

Heather lags behind me, seemingly unconcerned that Jacob's out of sight.

"I'll check the children's section," I call to her.

She simply nods, having not stepped inside the entrance yet.

I want to tell her to look with me. To at least check the other corners of this building. Maybe I'm overreacting. He's seven years old and quite clever. And this is a bookstore, not an especially hazardous locale. Maybe recent events are seeping into my psyche, painting the world as a much more dangerous place than it is.

Or maybe she's just a bad damned mother.

I slow a little on my way towards the children's area. My eyes catch a new true crime display, distracting me as I turn the corner. Since my eyes are stuck on the glossy covers adorning the end cap, I don't see the shelving stool that sits in my path. My feet betray me and I topple over the clutter. Before I hit the ground, a hand grabs my arm to break my fall and helps me upright.

My gaze meets a set of bright green eyes. I can't look away.

The man before me is handsome, with a youthful face just slightly covered in a rough layer of stubble and dark brown hair with thick, wavy peaks.

"Reading while walking can lead to serious injury." He gives me a playful smile and runs a hand through his voluminous hair.

"I'm so sorry. I feel like such a klutz. Thank you for the hand." I curtsy like an idiot and hope he doesn't see me blush immediately after. "I just got distracted by the new true crime display."

"Obsessed with true crime?" He asks.

"Guilty. I enjoy your classic fictional killers too. Thomas Harris is a personal favorite author of mine." I wouldn't normally publicize my enthusiasm for true crime. People tend to look at me funny and get turned off.

Not him though. He doesn't even flinch.

"Ah, *The Silence of the Lambs*," he says in an almost reminiscent way.

I start to relax. Reality pours back in. "My nephew took off into the store. Have you seen a super excited, nerdy, seven-year-old boy with shaggy hair about this high?" I mark Jacob's height, placing my hand a little above my waist, palm down.

The man doesn't look down at my hand. His eyes are locked on mine. After an intense moment, he breaks his eyes away and busies himself with straightening books. It's only then that I notice the name tag and realize he works here.

Adam.

"Sorry. I wish I could help you, but I haven't seen him," Adam says. "It's not the first time this has happened here. I'm sure he's okay, though, Probably sitting in a pile of books somewhere."

"I really should go looking for him."

"I'll make sure to not move the true crime display," he says with a smirk. Is he flirting with me?

I start backing away wishing I didn't have to leave when my phone rings. Heather's name glows on the screen. I answer.

"Did you find him?" I ask her before she has a chance to say anything.

"Yeah he was in the graphic novels section by the cafe."

I turn back to the man in the stacks. I don't want to say goodbye just yet.

"That's great. I'll be right over." I hang up the phone.

"The culprit's been found in the graphic novels section," I say to Adam. "He's here with his mom for a visit. I'd better go." I force myself to turn to leave, regretting it instantly, but still I struggle to take a step forward.

"Wait." He tugs at the sleeve of my jacket. I turn around and look at his face. He has such inviting green eyes. I get lost tracing the lines of his firm jaw down to his neck. His skin is tanned a healthy shade, a pleasant legacy from the summer sun. "I'm Adam. Adam Collins."

"Lydia... Walker." I say, flustered. I feel like this is what high school should have felt like as a wave of superficial nostalgia comes over me.

We awkwardly shake hands.

Adam says, "Would you like to..."

"Yes," I respond.

He chuckles. "You don't want to know what you're agreeing to?"

I shake my head in embarrassment. "What am I agreeing to?"

"Maybe a walk around the city?"

"Not quite what I was expecting... But it's still a yes... Wait here."

I walk over to the information desk, feeling his eyes on my back. I grab a free bookmark with a list of "Horror Required Reading". I write my number down on it and make the short walk back to him.

"A fan of horror too?" he asks.

"Kind of." I smirk. "It's not like I'm crazy for horror or anything. I only spend about a dozen hours a week watching horror films, and I've only read, like, thirty-seven of Stephen King's books."

"Oh, so you've never attended the Portland Horror Film Festival then? Or the H.P. Lovecraft one, right?" he asks with a sarcastic tone.

"I have no idea what you're talking about. And I certainly haven't already bought my ticket for next year." We laugh. "I really do need to go. They're waiting for me."

"Of course. It was nice to meet you, Lydia Walker. I'll call you."

"Looking forward to it."

As I walk away, I wonder what I'm more excited about: reading the updated profile on the serial killer or the fact that I just landed a date simply by talking about horror and true crime.

It's not a challenge to spot Jacob. He's sitting in the middle of the floor with graphic novels stacked up around him and one open in his lap. I sit down beside him.

"Couldn't decide on just one, huh?" I tease.

He looks up for a moment and sticks his tongue out. I search around for Heather, and my eyes catch her at the end of an aisle, checking her watch and pacing. She spots me and waves. Her phone rings and she turns her back to me when she answers it.

A few seconds later, she puts her hand over the phone and walks over to me.

"Can you watch Jacob for a few minutes? I need to take this." She hurries away before I can answer her.

I turn my attention to Jacob. "So, how have you been? Are you enjoying school this year? What are your friends like?"

"Yeah, I like to go to school. I wish I went every day," he says.

"What do you mean?" I try to keep my tone light.

"Sometimes we stay home and have cartoon days when mom doesn't wake up in time." He seems careful to only answer the question I ask and not give anything else away.

"How many times a week do you have cartoon days?" I ask.

"Ummm... one or two?" he replies, looking at me as if he's guilty of something. He clutches the graphic novel and starts tapping his feet on the ground.

"When you go to school, what do you do after you get home?"

"Sometimes I watch TV, play in my room, read comic books, or go outside." His eyes sparkle. A wide grin spreads over his face when he mentions going outside.

"With your mom?" I ask.

He winces and the glint in his eye fades. "She's there but she doesn't play with me."

"What does she do when you play then?"

"Watch TV mostly. Sometimes she just stares out the window... and ...." He turns his head away from me.

"You can tell me, Jacob. I can keep a secret."

He opens his mouth to speak, but hesitates. I haven't quite convinced him. I bring my hand to my mouth and act like I'm zipping it up and throwing away the key.

He giggles and moves closer. "Sometimes when I wake up after a bad dream, or when I have to go to the bathroom at night, mom is gone," he whispers in my ear.

I feel sick. I hope I'm wrong, but Jacob wouldn't lie about this. She's got to be using again. I don't think of heroin though. Not with what Jacob has said. I can't imagine her living a semi-normal life on heroin. I can figure it out through Jacob if I hurry. I don't want Heather to catch me talking to him about this.

"Jacob, when she gets back, does she seem happy or sad?"

"I don't know. She walks around the house all night though. It's hard to sleep."

"Yeah, when there's a lot of noise that does make it hard, huh?" I say, trying to keep the conversation casual.

"I just want to sleep. Sometimes I have funny dreams."

"I do too. Do you know if your mom takes medicine? Like how you take medicine when your nose is stuffy or your tummy hurts? And what does she do the day after being gone?" I don't want to ask him too many questions, but I know our time alone is short.

"Well, she yells more and walks around the house a lot. I think she calls the doctor because she's always on the phone. She tells him she needs it badly. I think it's the medicine for her scratching."

"Her scratching?"

"Mom tells me not to scratch when my skin itches, but she does it all the time."

"Jacob, you're doing a really good job. One more question. Does your mom work at your school?" I need to know how much she's been lying about.

"She did last year, but she stays home now."

There are so many questions I still want to ask, but I see Heather coming down the aisle. I whisper to Jacob, "Our secret," then point at a graphic novel from his pile in an attempt to not look suspicious and say, "This one looks good."

"Thanks for watching him," Heather says as she makes her way toward us. "It was important."

She offers no explanation of what was important, why she was gone so long, or who she was talking to. Her eyes dart around the store and she jiggles her bracelets. For a second, I think it's a nervous tick, but it's not. It's a twitch.

I'm about to ask her some roundabout questions when my phone rings. I mouth the word "sorry" as I stand.

"Your very important case?" Heather says.

"Most likely," I respond, ignoring how dismissive she sounds. As the phone continues ringing, I look down at Jacob and say, "I'll be right back, buddy."

He's already cracked open another graphic novel, too distracted to respond.

I walk over to a table in the cafe area and sit.

"Walker here," I say into the phone.

"There's been a development in the case," Frank says. "Can you come down to the station?"

"When?"

"Right now."

Frank's timing is crap. I glance over at Jacob. I really have missed him. Who knows when I'll get to see him next if I don't make the most of it while he's here, especially if Heather is as unstable as Jacob made her sound.

"It shouldn't take too long," Frank says, interrupting my thoughts.

"I can be down there within the hour. I was just having a coffee and looking over the newest version of Yates' profile."

"Want me to pick you up?"

"Actually I'm at McDowell's downtown near the station, so I can just walk over. Thanks, though."

"You and that bookstore," he snickers and hangs up the phone.

I walk back over to Heather and Jacob. Heather scowls at me, predicting what I'm about to say. "Let me guess," she jabs. "You have to go, right?"

"I'm sorry. There's some new development in the case and I got called in. I'm so glad we got to have dinner and come here together."

"Me too," Jacob mumbles, apparently not as distracted by the graphic novel as I thought.

"Hopefully we'll see you before we leave at the end of the week,"

Heather says, avoiding eye contact, trying not to sound bothered.

"What's your plan while you're here?"

"I thought you had to go," she snaps.

"I do, but I have a few minutes."

"I don't know yet. We can't stay too long. I have to go back to work eventually."

The corner of her mouth rises into a sickening grin. I glare at her and think of how it's so easy for her to lie to my face.

I tell her and Jacob goodbye and head for the exit. Not soon after I've left them, a pile of books falls to the ground behind me.

I know it's Heather who yells, "Now look what you did!"

Clenching my teeth, I keep walking. Her lies are ruining her life, and she's dragging Jacob down with her.

Chapter 12

ADAM

I feel so exhilarated when I get home. This time, I didn't just take instant photographs. I brought my favorite manual camera with me too. In the red glow of my dark room, I can see the gruesome images of terror and fear. But those emotions transform, mellowing into a peaceful death. The truth really did set them free. The photos of them zipped back up in their sleeping bags are so gratifying. I forced them to confront their demons. They'll emerge on the other side of this ordeal with a weight lifted off of them. The walls that held them prisoner will all fall away.

I did that for them.

I've seen my share of thriller films and read plenty of novels about killing. I've never understood the lack of control. I'm very aware of my urges and I know how to keep them in check. The way I choose to kill my victims gives me a level of intimacy I've never been able to find before. I don't seek out opportunities. They present themselves to me every day but it's only the really serious offenders that deserve to die.

It's been a few days since I revealed the truth to my latest prey, the Bakers. I wake up feeling well-rested as the late morning sun beams through my window. I get up and I make my way to McDowell's for my shift. I work from home most of the time, dealing rare books. Now and again it's nice to be exposed to new people, it's important for the hunt. I'm not going to work to look for victims, but if I come across someone who is an unremorseful liar, someone whose abusive lies damage the ones they *love,* I can't ignore it.

I was having a rather dull day until I met her.

I spent a while on the register, then moved to shelving. I saw one couple making out in the stacks and caught another attempting to shoplift. Nothing out of the ordinary until a thud startled me, jolting my attention toward a woman falling right beside me, close enough to catch.

And I did. Her eyes held my gaze long after, admitting that she was enamored with the true crime display.

It's only been a few minutes since she slipped a bookmark between my fingers, her name and number written on the thin card stock. I was too enamored by her to reveal much about myself, and I'm too cautious to let anyone in that easily. I think about her nervous laugh and her hesitation as she almost walked out of my life every bit as quickly as she had fallen into it. I couldn't bear to see her go, since I knew so little about her.

I know there's something more to her. She's a deep well holding secrets and sorrows too numerous to fathom. If she was willing to be open about her love for chilling fiction, I can only imagine what other devious details I might learn given more time.

I continue to shelve books, moving along to the next room when someone else catches my eye.

This girl is skinny, and she looks harried. There's something off about her. Maybe it's drugs, or maybe she just doesn't get enough sleep. Judging by the way she keeps checking her watch, it's possible that she's waiting for someone. I continue to watch out of the corner of my eye as her impatient loitering moves her over by the restrooms. Tapping her boot toe on the slab floor, she fiddles with the water bottles and idly inspects whatever merchandise is nearby.

A few minutes later, she sees the man she's been looking for. Most people would be excited to see him go. His hair is disheveled, and his rancid funk hits me from ten feet away. She moves in close to him and slips some folded up cash into his coat pocket. He in turn drops a bag of white powder into hers. I have to hand it to them—they're subtle. If they hadn't been facing away from the aisle I was shelving in I would have missed it entirely.

It would be so easy to choke the life out of her. Or to bring her close to me with one arm while I stabbed her deep in the chest with the other. The urge is there because she's weak, a junkie even, but I don't let myself lose control.

I wait for the sketchy man to walk away. He finally leaves and she rushes off in the other direction. I want to follow her, to scare her in some subtle way. Perhaps I could approach her with a friendly, "Can I help you find anything?" I'm surprised at how uncomfortable most people get when they receive this question from a stranger, even if that stranger is there to service their needs.

My brainstorming is cut short by a chorus of light *thuds* that I've heard a hundred times and know too well. A pile of books hitting the ground.

"Look at what you did!" a woman screams.

I head toward the commotion.

It's her again, standing in the middle of the graphic novel section, grabbing a young boy's arm and shaking it.

"I'm sorry, Mom I didn't mean to," the boy says.

Mom... A mother who buys drugs while her young child peruses through a bookstore.

"What are you waiting for? Pick them up!" she commands.

The kid braces himself, waiting for the back of her hand. When the smack doesn't come, he gets down on his hands and knees and picks up the fallen graphic novels. While he does this, she slides books over to him with her foot and kicks him a few times. Not hard, but enough to scare him.

"This is why I never take you anywhere." She glances in my direction. "See everyone looking at you?" she scolds the boy.

By my count, it's only me looking at them currently. She's shaming him to prove a point. I need to step in to say something. To stop this poor boy from being belittled and abused further by the person who should love him the most. I know how he feels all too well. I wish there had been someone to end my misery and the unhappiness I went through when I was his age.

She gets impatient and grabs him by the arm. "We're going back to the hotel."

"No!" the boy yells, making an even bigger scene. "Camping!"

She yanks him upward with no regard for the remaining mess.

"Camping!" the boy yells again.

His knees drag across the carpet as she carries him past me. I might as well not be here at all.

"We're not going camping," she says through clenched teeth.

"No!" the boy yells again.

If I was curious before, I'm fully invested now.

"Ma'am," I call to her. "We have guides in the travel section. I'm sure we could find you and your boy a place to camp."

The boy finds his footing and stands upright. Even as he tries to rip his arm away from his mother, he beams.

She stares blankly at me, and I know what she's thinking—my offer got her son to shut up.

"Where's the travel section?" she says.

"Yes," the boy whispers.

I lead them to the aisle. She plops the boy down on a bench with her palms pressed against his shoulder. "Now, just sit here and be quiet."

"I can help you get started with a few ideas," I say, if for no other reason than to take her focus away from the child.

"We don't have a lot of money, so we'll have to camp somewhere cheap," she says.

Lies. She *would* have the money if she wasn't so weak. I'm sure she'd find some money to get her fix. If only she would realize that the welfare of her son should be held above all else. I refuse to turn my back on this, especially with how abusive she is towards him. He doesn't deserve to grow up like this. If she is going to treat him with such disregard, she doesn't deserve him. She doesn't deserve a life at all. All she wants is to get high, to live from score to score. She isn't going to get that now.

"We're visiting," she says. "You know these guidebooks, right? Save me some time."

"I know of a few places. Some aren't in these travel books though. There's a few in Washington across the river."

"That might be nice. Different, at least. I explored a lot of Oregon when I lived here."

"You should check out the Clickitaw Wildlife Area," I tell her. "It's not too far. You can camp at a place called the Dellacain Canyon Unit. Just put in Milepost 5 and Highway 142 in your navigation. It'll get you there. It's right along the Clickitaw River."

"Do you know if it has free admission this weekend?" she asks.

"It's free all year. Not very many tourists even know about it. It's very secluded." Perfect for me.

"I was thinking of somewhere with more people. You know, so he's got some other kids to play with."

Like a family that could babysit her son while mommy gets in a pocket of powder and goes out of her head. Selfish bitch.

"I think since this is so last minute those campgrounds will probably be full or at the very least require a two-night stay," I say. "Plus they charge."

I almost have her. This moment is almost as good as sticking the knife in for the first time.

"Can we go, Mom? Please?" the boy asks.

"Stop whining, Jacob," she barks. "Where is it again?"

"It's about five and a half miles northeast of Lyle. Here, I'll show you."

I take her phone for a moment and put in the coordinates to make sure she won't get lost.

"Thanks," she says with not the slightest amount of excitement.

"I know you said you'd be here in Portland for a little while longer," I say. “But if I were you, I'd go camping tomorrow to cheat the weather.”

“What do you mean?”

“After tomorrow, we’re going to get rain all during the next ten days. You’ve gotta love that Oregon weather. It’s changing all the time. Just never for the better.” I give a goofy grin to seal the lie.

“I guess that makes sense then. Thanks. We'll try and go tomorrow.”

They both walk away from me and out of the store. This will be the first time I give anyone so much lead time. I'm letting this pair go on their way. I won’t follow them. The time will pass slowly for me—time in between meeting my prey and killing them. This campground is only a few hours away. I can take my time and go after them later.

A rush of confidence swells inside of me. I thumb the corner of the bookmark nestled in my pocket and can only think to channel the excitement in one way. I pull out my phone.

No. It’s too soon to call Lydia. The time on my phone confirms it. I have to be patient and ride this high until the time is right.

Chapter 13

LYDIA

If not for the impromptu briefing and my sour interaction with Heather, my lips would be open wide, bearing a cheesy smile. I have a date. At least, I think I do. It's completely possible—realistic, even—that Adam tossed that bookmark in a trashcan as soon as I left McDowell's.

Something tells me he didn't, though. The moment I met him, I felt that there was something indescribable between us. It was in the way our eyes locked onto one another. I felt it through my whole body.

It would be the only date I've had for over a year and the first one in multiple years that I'm actually looking forward to.

As I walk through the Portland PB halls, only part of my subconscious registers I'm here. Another, more optimistic, version of me is dreaming of walking along the Portland sidewalks, with my dark stranger stealing glances at me from my side.

My daydream doesn't last for long, though, as images of Heather, weathered and frail, replace the serene environment—a collage of her present self and the one I saw by the dumpster all those years ago merging into one. As long as she's in Portland, dragging Jacob around like some burdensome growth she's eager to remove, I'm not sure I'll be at peace.

I wish there was something I could do to pull Jacob away from her. She's teetering on the edge of something that will irrevocably damage him. Like I was damaged. Eventually, he'll see through her secrets.

Eventually, she'll have to answer for her lies.

Maybe that's why I understand this killer. He has a clear reason for killing these people. The scenes are littered with messages of his conviction. Even those victims who are innocent are better off dead, like those boys. Part of me wishes that someone would have put me out of my misery before I had the chance to become this lonely, twisted person. If someone had killed my parents for their sins, and they had killed me as well, I wouldn't have had to suffer all those years before I was even a teenager.

I enter the conference room and spot Frank sitting in the same seat he took just hours before. A true creature of habit. I take the seat next to him and wait for Detective Harshaw, who paces a few feet below us. Looking around the room at all of these police officers, detectives, and representatives of different agencies, I know they won't understand what I do now. They can't understand how I see things now.

Finally, Harshaw begins his briefing. "Thank you, everyone, for coming in at the last minute. We've had the opportunity to ask some questions after obtaining the credit card statements of the victims from both crimes. With that info, we've started to discreetly canvas the areas where both the first and second sets of victims were during their last hours. The updated profile, which I don't expect you to have read in the last few hours, discusses our latest theory. The killer most likely met his victims in a store, or some other public place, so we're currently retracing their steps. Tourists tend to pay with debit or credit cards when traveling. This will be of great help to us in establishing their routes.

"The first two victims, Eric Black and Kasey Hill, were staying at a hotel downtown. They also obtained a rental car near the airport. The credit card statement shows that their last purchase occurred in an outdoor goods store in downtown Portland. They may have gone other places, or used cash, but we're going to send officers over there to take some statements. Maybe some employees will remember them. With any luck, they might even have noticed something out of the ordinary or can recall an encounter the victims may have had in the store with someone out of place, or strange in some way.

"The Baker family will be more difficult to track since they visited almost a dozen locations on the morning of their murder alone. We are going to follow up with the staff from their hotel and the rental car company that their vehicle comes from. One pattern that can be discerned is that both pairs of victims checked out of their hotels, rented cars, and headed far away to destinations that would prove to be the sites of their deaths. These victims headed for free campgrounds that were hardly known outside local circles, and each was several hours' drive from their hotels. We need to find him before he kills again. There are too many free camping sites throughout the state for us to keep track of them all." With that, Harshaw stops pacing and crosses his arms, as if waiting for questions.

With the briefing over, the room is empty with the exception of Frank and me. Between his furrowed brows, he narrows his eyes at me.

"What's going on up there?" he asks gently, prodding the side of my head with his index finger.

"It's just all so fascinating," I say. When he answers that with a frown, I quickly add, "I mean, I know people are dead, but I'm fascinated by the reasons he's communicating to us. We have all the pieces to figure out *why* he's killing these particular people, and it's... interesting."

"I've been a detective for a long time," Frank says, "and I've never seen a serial killer. Even though this kind of case is exceedingly rare, I still can't find anyone fascinating if their fantasies have them taking the lives of others. It's grotesque and horrible. My interest is in putting a stop to it."

"But he thinks they deserve it," I say meekly.

"They were just living their lives the best way they could. Maybe they were doing some things to harm themselves. But they weren't hurting others."

"Come on, Frank," I say sharply. He can't possibly be this simple-minded. "Sure they were. Their actions would have had serious consequences in the future. Those boys may have grown up miserable and traumatized by what their mother was doing to their family. They may have gone on to have one failed relationship after another, perpetuating the cycle of lies and abuse. We don't know."

"You're right. We don't know. And he took away any chance of us ever finding out."

"The actions of one person create ripples through their lives," I counter. "We can't track everything, can't predict exactly how these boys would have coped. But we can make educated guesses. Even the people involved can't understand the full impact of their actions."

Frank looks at me in a way I've never seen before. I can't quite make it out. Disappointment, shock, disgust maybe. I don't really care.

"There's a lot about my past that you don't know, Frank," I say.

"It's not for lack of trying. You're a closed book."

"There's a reason for that. Sometimes the past can be so damning that it haunts you your whole life. Someone with a past like that counts themselves lucky for the scarce seconds and minutes when they aren't thinking about the abuse. They're forever grateful whenever they get a reprieve from those memories. Mentioning any of it aloud is about the worst way to forget it. It would just make things worse." I'm shaking when I stop speaking.

Frank shakes his head dismissively and turns away.

"I may not know what you've been through," he says, "but I still don't understand how you can respect a serial killer. This one in particular. And Lydia... I understand perfectly well how painful the past can be."

He gets up and walks out of the room. Part of me wants to say something—but what can I say? The truth is this killer is waking me up and pulling me out of the dreadful existence that I was trapped in for years. I'm not giving that up for anyone.

Chapter 14

ADAM

Just before closing, I dial the number scrawled on the bookmark.

"Hello?" Lydia says from the other end.

I'm weakened by her voice. That rush of confidence I've felt for hours fails me. "It's Adam... from McDowell's," I say.

"I'm glad you clarified," she teases. "I mean, I could have met dozens of Adams in the past half hour."

"I remember you mentioning that you had family in town, but didn't know if you had any time tomorrow? Earlier in the day, maybe, to... walk around the city?" My breathing is a little too quick and I hope she's not picking it up on her end.

"I'm actually off work tomorrow for the first time in a while. And, no, I don't have any plans."

"Is that a yes then?" I ask.

"Yes, um... I'm sorry... I'm a bit drained. Work stuff."

Her exhaustion is evident through the speaker.

"Don't be sorry. Let's meet at the Rose Gardens downtown and we can walk from there."

"You know, I've lived here for years and still I've never been there," she admits.

"We'll fix that tomorrow. Meet me by the information stand. Does ten work for you?" I ask.

I'm worried that with Lydia I'm already at ease. My guard is coming down too quickly. I have to be careful. Keep some distance. A few hours together, then we'll part and I'll prepare for tomorrow night's festivities.

"Ten works. I'll make sure to bring my camera. I've heard the place is gorgeous."

"You're a photographer?"

There's a brief pause before she says in a monotone voice, "There's a lot you don't know about me." She laughs nervously. "That was so lame. I'm sorry."

We chat for a few more minutes. With every word spoken, I become even more attracted to her.

Tomorrow's going to be a good day.

I couldn't sleep last night. I just lay in bed anticipating this morning.

I'm sitting on a bench in the luscious rose gardens, the strap of my camera around my neck, busily thinking about Lydia. And thinking about the fate of the woman I met yesterday. I won't know until later this afternoon if I was convincing enough. Maybe I should have waited to go on a date with Lydia. After tonight, things will be a bit clearer, easier to work around. My mind is a whirlwind of conflicting thoughts. I'm darting back and forth between Lydia and my next kill. The real estate of my imagination is fractured into two fantasies. I'm busily imagining holding Lydia and kissing her full lips. I can remember the way they parted the smallest bit when she smiled at me. The imagery fades and Lydia is replaced by the deadbeat addict of a mother. She's still in my grasp, looking into my eyes piteously while I push the knife deep into the small of her back.

"I thought I was supposed to find you by the information stand," Lydia says over my shoulder, wrenching me free from my daydream.

She's dressed in slim black pants, a loose white V-neck shirt, and a jean jacket covered in buttons and pins. A stiff leather bag sits at her hip, connected at each end by a slightly worn leather strap that runs across her body and over her shoulder. I understand it to be a camera bag. Her head is blocking the sun. Bursts of light shoot out in all directions around her, as if coming from her.

"I'm sorry," I say. "I guess I lost track of time. If it's any consolation, I was here early. I lost track of time daydreaming about you."

This makes her smile, and a wave of heat rises through me.

"You're a photographer too?" she asks, eyeing the camera that all of a sudden feels light in my hands.

"Amateur," I answer.

"I prefer the term enthusiast," she says. "Come on." She bobs her head, motioning for me to go with her toward the garden, and I realize I'm still sitting.

I check my watch.

"Technically our date doesn't start for another five minutes," I say.

"Suit yourself." She turns quickly and starts walking to the far side of the garden, knowing I'd walk after her. So I do.

At the end of a row, she doubles back and weaves her way toward some bright orange blooms. She leans far over, lifting one foot centimeters above the ground, and pulls one blossom close to her nose. She locks eyes with me as she savors the odor.

For a moment, we're the only two people in the rose garden. I hold my camera in my hands and raise it to my face. Through the tiny viewfinder, I find her and capture her. I let go of the camera and it bobs on the strap hanging around my neck. She takes the camera out of her bag and snaps a quick shot of me. Before she can steal another, I put my hand in front of my face playfully.

"I see how it is," she chides. "You can take photos of me, but I can't have any of you. That's not fair at all. At least let me see it."

She tugs on my strap to bring me down to her height. We are so close that our noses are almost touching. I feel the warmth of her hands against my skin as she raises the strap over my head so she can look at the camera.

She takes the camera and starts to scan the last few shots I took. The last one is of her smelling the rose. Before that, a few of the rose garden I took while I waited for her. My thoughts trail off as I think of the photos that come before that. Did I remember to change out the memory card since I used it at Mineral Falls? My heart starts to race. I put a hand on the camera, my fingers touching hers.

"Well, if you get to see mine, I get to see yours too." I reach out for her camera. She takes a quick step back from my reach.

She lets out a quick laugh. "Sorry. For a second, I had to remember whether I changed out the memory card. I definitely did."

It's like she's in my head. "You got sensitive material in there?" I ask. "There *is* a lot I don't know about you, isn't there?"

She giggles.

"What line of work are you in?" I ask.

"I'm a forensic photographer for the Portland Police Bureau. I also help out with the forensic sciences program at the University of Oregon. But the majority of my experience comes from the different crime scenes that I spend time at." I sense her shrinking away as she says this, almost as if she's ashamed.

"So you have to see some gruesome stuff?"

"Yeah... Every now and again I'm called in for a break in or something mundane. But sometimes it's homicides."

Homicides... Portland Police Bureau... There's no way my luck could be that bad.

"Hm." I nod my head. "Seems like a great pairing since you like true crime so much."

She tilts her head. "Usually people don't act this casually when I tell them I take pictures of dead bodies."

"Someone's gotta do it, right?" I say plainly. "Might as well be an amateur detective."

I begin to walk down the row of flowers, and she follows, softening.

"I never said I was an amateur detective," she says.

And now it's time for me to find out whether she's been part of my investigation. "So you've been on a case lately, have you?"

She hesitates. I'm sure there are strict limits to what she can tell me. I'm hoping she doesn't give me enough to end this now. It's possible that we might both possess photos of the deceased Baker family.

"Yeah," she says. "Normally I deal with standalone crimes, though."

"And they let you walk away with the photos? I mean, I just thought they would be in evidence, or lockup or something like that." As I say this, she flushes.

"How long have you been working at McDowell's?" she asks.

Damn. If she *is* assigned to my case, I won't know today. I wonder if the Portland PB has given me a nickname. The Campsite Killer, maybe?

"I only work at McDowell's part-time," I say. "I fill in for people when they're out sick and when they're on vacation. I run my own small business, which can get pretty lonely, so McDowell's gives me a chance to work with people face-to-face. And, of course, the people-watching can be very entertaining."

"Yes, it's much better than T.V. I'm sure that employee discount doesn't hurt either."

We round the bend along the main brickwork path and crest the hill above the amphitheater.

"You should see my library," I say. "I've been collecting books for years. It's kind of depressing to think that I'll be dead long before I could ever read them all."

"I'm the same way," Lydia says. "I finish one book and add three more to my shelves. McDowell's is an addiction of mine."

"Then you might be interested to know that I'm a rare book dealer."

"That's your small business?"

"Sure is. I had a storefront years ago, but now it's all done online. It usually involves a lot of restoration and preservation, but sometimes I get to travel."

"That is... *so* cool." The expression on her face is one of pure admiration. It's as if I just told her that I'm saving the lives of children. Or that I'm a scientist working on some groundbreaking cure. I've never gotten such a sweet reaction to book preservation. It's refreshing. As a boy, I had always been teased for reading so much. If I was ever caught reading by my aunt or uncle, they would rip the book out of my hands and throw it in the garbage.

Lauren never valued my career. She could only be bothered to read on the rare occasion that she pulled herself away from her phone. I'd show her a particularly good example of some rare volume and she'd stop what she was doing for a moment, give it a cursory look, smile and nod, then go back to whatever tweeting or surfing she was engaged in. And the times when she would try to convey fake excitement were even worse. In front of me, right now, is a woman who seems truly fascinated by my career and by my life.

Lydia leans in and says, "I'm obsessed with books. Honestly, it's probably unhealthy." She laughs. "I have to visit every single bookstore I pass. Sometimes I find myself in the classics section picking up and opening different books, not to read them but to smell them. I've bought books for their weathered, earthy smell."

And I love that smell as well.

"Even before I became a rare book dealer," I say, "I had stacks of old novels and plays. There's something hauntingly beautiful about an author being able to live on forever through their work. I write a little too. I find it therapeutic."

"I write too. Mostly short stories and poetry. Just to do it."

"Because you enjoy it."

"Yeah. Because I enjoy it."

We smile at each other.

Softly, I ask her, "Are you enjoying this?"

Her smile widens, and she answers, "I am."

This could be very stupid of me. Possibly reckless. I have no idea if she's been walking through the aftermath of murders. Frankly, as I get lost in her eyes, I don’t have the sense of mind to care.

There is much to be done this afternoon, I know there is. But in this moment, any sense of worry and anticipation disappears into her smile. I grab her hand and run my fingers lightly over her palm. I don't want to let go.

Chapter 15

LYDIA

I don't want to let go.

He grabs me by the shoulders and pulls my face close to his. I can feel his breath on my cheek. He moves my chin to his face and gives me a brief, gentle kiss. When he begins to pull away, I just can't help myself. I kiss him hard, running my fingers up his arms, around his shoulders, and through his hair.

I pull away to meet his eyes and exhale. His eyes widen and his mouth hangs half open. He tries to collect himself, the heat of his breath warming my cheeks.

He moves his mouth down to my neck, kissing me so lightly it's almost as if it didn't happen. I close my eyes and let the subtle shocks plunge from my neck to my feet.

He stops and laughs into my neck, then embraces me. "I almost forgot we're in public," he says.

"I have a few things to sort out over the next few days, but I'll call you later this week," Adam tells me.

It's been nearly two hours since we began walking through the garden. I knew this date would end one of two ways: I get an urgent call from the bureau, or he ends it. I could live this morning forever.

He steps toward me and I'm reliving our kiss all over again, savoring it as my eyes close involuntarily.

When I open my eyes, he's already walking away. I look down at my feet. He's sprinkled multicolored rose petals all around me. The decoration holds me in my place like a salt ring, trapping me. Protecting me. I scan up the path and see him looking at me from the far side of the garden with those intense green eyes before he disappears through hedges.

I stand there for a long time, going over every part of the morning in my mind. I pick up a few handfuls of the petals and press them between my fingers. Their silken fragility holds my attention as I try not to bruise them. More people are showing up at the rose gardens, but I don't want to leave. As long as I stay, the morning is real.

I find a bench and sit, pulling my battered paperback of *The Silence of the Lambs* out of my camera bag. I thumb it open. Every few minutes I catch myself losing my place on the page, glancing up at the garden and all the different places we walked together. I stare at the spot where we kissed and close my eyes to relive it slowly.

Reality jerks me out of my daydream with the vibrating pulse of my phone.

A picture text from Jacob—his smiling face in the foreground, his mother is at the wheel over his shoulder. Blurred foliage whips past them outside of the car.

I text him back: "Nice selfie! Where are you two going?"

I wait as the ellipsis dances at the bottom of my screen.

His response appears. "Camping."

My stomach sinks at the sight of the word. Mere seconds later, I have the phone to my ear, waiting for him to pick up.

"Hi, Aunt Lydia!" he yells over the wind whistling behind him.

"Jacob, could you put your mom on the phone please?" I say hurriedly.

"Mom, Aunt Lydia wants to talk to you," he says.

I wait.

"Hey, Lydia," Heather says.

"Jacob says you're going camping?" I ask.

"Jealous? I would've invited you, but I figured you'd be busy."

I can't reveal any details about my case. "Heather..." Screw it. Who's she going to tell? "Heather... campers have..." I lower my voice, careful to not be overheard by pedestrians. "... died."

"Oh, shit."

Jacob shrieks from beyond the receiver. "Mommy said a bad word!"

She ignores it. "You know how much Jacob likes the outdoors."

"Then go canoeing or paddleboarding or anything else."

"I can handle myself, Lydia." She pronounces my name in such a venomous way that I know I've already lost the argument. I know what she means. I know that in the days between her parents burning to death and her finally getting clean, she felt alone, forced to be independent and fend for herself.

What she doesn't acknowledge—what she's *never* acknowledged—is that I'm the one who dug her out of that pit. I don't think she even remembers or cares that I'm the reason Jacob is still in her life and not stuck in foster care. She would have had her parental rights severed if she wasn't able to get her shit together through my help and months of expensive rehab.

So, no, she *can't* take care of herself.

But there's no point in fighting if she won't listen. All I can do is warn her, for Jacob's sake. "Please just be careful," I say. "Make sure wherever you go isn't isolated. Make sure the campground is densely populated."

"Yeah, sure," she says.

"Promise me, Heather."

"Yeah, I promise," she says flatly. "Thanks for the concern."

The line goes dead.

She would fit so nicely within the group of liars and their loved ones. The relapsed drug addict who spits on every opportunity to improve herself. Who neglects her child, her job, and any responsibilities.

But that's just paranoia setting in. Heather and Jacob are but two out of hundreds of campers all over Portland.

Chapter 16

ADAM

I'm only an hour from the campground. The Clickitaw Wildlife area is massive, but I was smart enough to lure her to a specific area: Dellacain Canyon. Recalling the directions I gave to the junkie, I know I have to get to the West side of the river.

I regularly make small cash withdrawals from my business account, so I always have enough cash on hand when I need it. Earlier, I stopped in Lyle, only five miles away, and bought an old pickup truck for a few hundred. I hope the damn thing makes it back into town. Lyle has just over five hundred residents so if you were to blink at the wrong time you could drive right through it and miss the whole thing. I leave my car in Lyle behind an abandoned building and walk six blocks to my temporary truck. I can't have anyone finding my tire tracks around the crime scene even though I always park far away from the campground.

I still don't need to take any unnecessary risks. Uncertainty like that is what keeps me up at night. I'm sure by now they've linked my first two crimes. It's pretty clear they're being investigated together; there's been nothing about either of them in newspapers or anywhere online. I've kept a pretty watchful eye on the crime beat columns. The police wouldn't want harmful information like that floated out to the public. If they publicized the two crimes or released any information about my six victims, it would lead to statewide hysteria, especially in a case where they have no leads. If this one shows up next it will be even more confusing for them. I'll leave the detectives scratching their heads while they stand around drinking their stale coffee. You don't think it is an accident that my next kill is in Washington, do you?

My guess is that by now they've involved the Portland Police Bureau and maybe even brought in the FBI on the case. If my next set of victims is across state lines, in Washington, I'll be adding another agency into the mix. They're really not known for strong interagency cooperation. They can be quite territorial with crime scenes and with information. It won't make anyone look good in Oregon if they're giving tips or case files to Washington crime officials. Even to make them aware of a serial killer might be considered disloyal. If I'm lucky, this will further slow progress on the case. For some detectives, solving cases is their bread and butter, but for others, it's just a bumpy road to small-time fame. Most likely, my greatest ally will be miscommunication between agencies, which is fine by me.

These amusing thoughts calm me as I enter the Clickitaw Wildlife Area. I drive past my turn and scope out the Dellacain Canyon Unit to see if they've arrived. I'm still for a few minutes until a car flies past me. To the north, all I can see beyond the road is the endless repetition of tree trunks. They fade deep into the forest where the strangling of the light makes any further distinction impossible. On the other side of the road is a great field, sweeping and barren, sparse with bushes and plants that angles down a slight grade into the valley south of us.

I come up to the area and don't see any cars or people from my vantage on the road.

Damn it.

To date, this is the most careless I've been. Not only do I not know if they're coming at all, but I have no clue what kind of car she'll be driving. I know exactly how it happened. It was right after I met Lydia, which makes sense. I was blunted, made a careless leap on too little information, and now I've opened myself up to a potentially dangerous scenario.

I pull the truck over and yank the parking brake. I tell myself not to worry. They'll show. I take a few deep breaths and peer at the valley to help clear my thoughts. I shut my eyes and think back to running my fingers through Lydia's hair, and how natural it felt to press my lips to hers. I feel more at peace already. She may have led me into carelessness, but at this moment her image is able to bring me some clarity.

I pull the truck back onto the winding road and make a quick U-turn to head back. I have to drive over to the West side of the Clickitaw River since the campsite is on the East bank. I turn down Fisher Hill Road and pass houses topped with moss-eaten roofs, getting a look at the lives of their inhabitants as I drive past. I start to think about the residents inside. Two kids use a swing set in the back of one house, and a woman looks at them through the kitchen window. The driveway is empty. The father must still be at work. After years of marriage, do they have dinner together every night? Or do they take their plates into their separate sanctums to eat in silence? Is their communication limited to brief formulaic exchanges at the beginning and end of every day? Do they share a happy life, and do their children get the love and attention they deserve?

Probably not.

Past the last house in the row, there's a vast tract of farmland and an asphalt bridge beyond. This is the only indicator I'll get to help me find the Clickitaw Trail, which leads me down to the river. By the time I reach the edge of the river, I'll hopefully have sight of them through my binoculars.

I don't see a soul at Dellacain, but now I'll have time to prepare for their arrival.

The campsite is surrounded by oaks. They tower over the whole area, providing shade. Beyond the forest, there's grassland that stretches and rolls out of view. This site is like the others. I've got a body of water to approach by, and the whole thing is not far from a seldom-used dusty backroad. No one would hear her scream here, but I'm not letting it come to that. I won't be giving her the chance to cry out or to beg for her life or the life of her son.

I skulk away from the river's edge, moving from tree to tree so I can remain unseen, on the rare chance that someone might be passing by. With each new tree, I stop to scope out the wooded area across the river. I need to pinpoint the intersection that I have given her. From this section of the river, it's all pretty convincing as an empty campground. Clinging to the third tree, I know I have found the spot. I load my map on my phone to be certain. I'm right across from where they will pull in off the road, if they ever arrive. I take shelter in an alcove so I won't be seen and stare at the temperamental river and the swaying branches of the trees. I lean against a root and brush some dirt off my head as I pull a paperback out of my bag and begin to read, hoping to be interrupted by the sounds of their arrival. A few pages into reading, I hear the unmistakable sounds of travel coming from far off. I lean my head out of my recess, towards the river, in an effort to listen more effectively. A car pulls off of the dirt road and into the camp area. Two car doors slam.

I jump to my feet as eager as a child who's just heard the bell announcing the end of a long school day. I peer through my binoculars and wait for the dust cloud to settle around their car. There they were. With a shock, I realize that I didn't even know if she would be bringing along a third person. I'm relieved to see just the two of them. The river is calm at the moment, and I can just barely make out their conversation. I have to remain far enough away.

I crawl up the embankment and settle back down on the ground, craning my neck around a tree trunk. My camera clicks away, dispensing photos as the scene unfolds.

"Mom, this is so cool," he tells her with excitement, marveling at the luscious wilderness surrounding him and the river between us.

"I'm glad. Now you can stop saying you've never been camping," she replies, annoyed.

He stands stark still in the middle of the clearing and asks, "Where's the bathroom?"

"There isn't one." She pops the trunk of the car and starts unpacking. She sure didn't bring much. Through my binoculars, I spot two sleeping bags, a tent, a few blankets, and a cooler.

"Where do I go then?" he asks.

"Out there in the woods." She points. "You dig a hole, and you find a leaf. Remember kiddo, you're the one who wanted to come out here."

"Okay," he mumbles, still looking quite lost. His eyes dart to the surrounding trees and then back to his mother.

"What are you staring at? Do you need my help going to the bathroom? You're so helpless." She grabs him by the arm. He loses his footing, but she doesn't give him a chance to regain his balance and starts dragging him over to a denser patch of trees and shrubs, a patch that I just so happen to be very close to.

"Mom, stop it! You're hurting me," he cries out.

She's moving closer to me with every resentful step. I lower to my stomach, and I believe I'm safe from her sight. At this distance, she won't be able to make me out, concealed as I am by some low growth at the base of a tree.

She flings him on the ground and draws back her arm. He braces for impact and collides to the ground with a *crunch*. It's not the sound of a broken bone or snapped twig. As he sobs on the ground, he removes something white, boxy, and plastic from his pocket. A chunk of it breaks off from the whole.

"My camera," he whimpers.

The woman lowers her hand. His pitiful cries might be what stops her from hitting him.

"I'll get you another one," she says, showing some semblance of humanity. But that humanity leaves just as soon as it appears. "Don't come back until it's dark. Show me you can take care of yourself for once." She walks away.

I watch him lower to the ground and curl up in a fetal position. I swing my binoculars over to the mother, now by the car. She rummages through her bag in a panic, tossing the contents of her purse over her shoulder frantically, when she comes upon the small plastic bag filled with white powder. In an instant, she's become as still as a statue, holding the bag tightly in one hand. She looks out along the trail, to where she left her son, and then her eyes fix on the bag. Quickly, she empties some of the drug onto the hood of her car. Laying her head down low by the small pile, she snorts.

After she does another hit, she throws her head back, closes her eyes, and gives a blind, buzzed smile.

The world will be better without her in it. The traumas her son has to face because of her won't leave him when he becomes an adult. He will be a broken person, carrying around the neglect, the abuse, and the feelings of abandonment and rejection. What's the alternative to killing him? He'd just end up in a foster home, primed for further abuse or with some uncaring distant relative. It's time to bring him peace and rid the world of this unfit mother.

The window of opportunity will close very rapidly. Since the mother left her son by the trees, I can drug him while I stalk the cokehead. It may be the only time that the two are separated. I'm about to cross the river a few meters downstream from where I last saw the boy. The waters are calmer there and littered with large rocks. Wide banks define the section keeping it shallow. I hear her call out to him in raspy hurried spurts.

"You better help me get this damn tent set up!" the mother yells from afar.

The boy's been laying in place for twenty minutes, doing as he's told, while his mother paces around the fire she's lit, chain-smoking cigarettes. The sun's nearly down, taking any warmth with it and making way for the chill of night. It's not completely dark out yet, but if I don't get to him soon, this could become very challenging. I scan the area through my binoculars.

The boy has barely moved since she left him. Maybe he fell asleep. I take a photo of him lying on the ground and he doesn't react to the noise of the camera. I recall how he looked when he first arrived. The sunlight was passing through leaves, casting his face in gold. He was looking up at the trees with excitement and fascination, and, as quick as the click of a shutter, his smile vanished. It was so easy for his mother to take away his happiness with no regard to his feelings or how her actions would impact him.

My face burns hot with rage. I tense my hands, then my forearms, my biceps, my shoulders, and I breathe out as I slowly relax them. I can control myself for a bit longer. She needs to die. The boy will finally be released from the grief he's experienced.

Once more glance through my binoculars shows me that the mother is on her hands and knees, facing away from me, fiddling with the cloth and metal of a tent aimlessly, the cocaine working to make her movements quick and jittery.

She won't see what I'm about to do.

I slide the photograph of the sleeping boy in a side compartment of my bag, then stuff the camera back inside of it, feeling for the rope to ensure it's accessible. With gloved hands, I get out a rag and soak it to excess with chloroform. I approach the boy while he's faintly snoring. I press the rag against his nose and mouth, watching as his eyes pop open. His body flails helplessly. He rolls to his back, fading into a deep sleep once more.

The ruined camera lies in two pieces next to the boy—a low-cost instant camera from what I can tell. Something he cared for deeply, now in disrepair.

Adrenaline courses through me as I whisper, "Consequences."

I rise up, taking careful footsteps toward the mother. With one turn, she could spot me, though, I'm hoping her drug-fueled daze will do its part in occupying her awareness. She seems awfully invested in doing a poor job at setting up that tent.

Twenty feet away...

Then fifteen...

Then ten...

And then it happens. She whips around, her mouth open, preparing for another angry yell—a yell that dives back into her throat at the sight of me.

I charge at her, making first contact with the edge of my shoulder. She's driven forward into her tent-in-progress and falls to the ground, hard. With one hand clapped over her mouth I wrench her upright. I switch hands and enfold her face in the sopping wet rag. I don't bother lowering her body to the ground.

She struggles until she doesn't.

With appropriate carelessness, I withdraw my arms and let gravity yank her downward. The resonant thud she makes on the packed earth is incredibly satisfying.

I jog back to the boy and throw all fifty-or-so pounds of him over my shoulder. I carry him over to the fire and ruined tent and lay him down a few feet away from his mother. I put his hands behind his back and bind them, then I tie his feet together. I make certain he's secure and gag him.

I wrap his mother's hands in rope, pull them behind her back, and tie her legs together. I then join her two sets of limbs with another length of cord. I want to be able to move her around easily and this gives me the option to pick her up by her hands and feet simultaneously. I search through her pockets and find one empty plastic bag and two that are full of white powder. The baggies fit easily in the palm of my hand. This is the last high she'll ever feel.

Let's make it count.

The boy is coming to, and almost immediately the tears begin streaming down his cheeks. He tries to spit out the gag, but I've taped it in place over his mouth. He moans and stomps his feet, trying to wake his mother. Her head lolls on lazy shoulders. Her unfocused eyes land on me first, then dart to the boy as he stomps the earth next to her. The eyes gain clarity with each passing second. She's starting to analyze her predicament. A confused terror registers on her face as she turns back to me. I don't understand the confusion that these people feel. It surprises me every time.

"Why are you so confused?" I ask. "You can't begin to imagine why someone would want you dead, right?"

She attempts a reply, but, of course, I can't understand anything she's saying through the gag. It's tempting to deny her the chance, but then again it could be amusing to hear what ramblings her addled brain might come up with.

I rip off the tape, but before I remove the gag, I wrap my fingers around her neck. "If you scream or call out for help, I'll kill you. Nod your head if you understand."

She nods. I take the gag out and wait for her response.

"What did I ever do to you?" she asks between gasps of air.

Even now part of her thinks this is all a game and that she'll actually live through it. What a conceited bitch.

"It's not what you've done to me. It's what you're doing to him." The boy reminds me so much of myself at his age that it's proving extremely difficult to stay in control.

"He has a roof over his head and food to eat," she says. "At least he has a parent. I lost mine when I was eight. Growing up in foster homes was a shitty way to—"

"You'll get no sympathy from me. You'd think that since you lost your parents, you of all people would understand that a child needs more than food and shelter. He needs your love and acceptance and support to have any chance at being happy in this life. Don't you understand that?"

"That's such bullshit. He's a strong little bastard. I was surprised that he made it at all since I was a junkie during the pregnancy."

"So, you don't use it anymore?"

"I've been clean for years now."

Her last remark sets me off. How can she lie so obviously and easily?

"There's no point in lying to me," I say, carefully withdrawing the small plastic bag from my pocket.

I hold it between my thumb and forefinger. Giving it a little jiggle in the air between us, I toss it against her face. With about a gram occupying the bag, it lands with a light *pat*. Would a gram be enough to kill her?

First, I need to kill the boy and make her watch.

I take one of my uncle's switchblades out of my back pocket and flip it open, staring down at this disgraceful creature with malice in my gaze. I lean over and grab her by the hair, twisting her neck toward her son. She won't get to escape a single second of this. "It's time for you to experience some fraction of the pain that you've caused him."

"He doesn't deserve to die because I'm a fuck up!" she belts. "I may not love him the way I should... And, yeah, I'm a shitty mom, okay! Let us go! I'll stop using. I'll go back to rehab. I'll figure out how to un-fuck life. I won't say anything, I swear. I won't say shit!"

The begging is unexpected, but she should know there's no way I can trust her to do any of the things she's saying. Just like she should know there's no way out of this.

I step forward and land a boot between her shoulder blades. While she writhes under me I lean over and tape the gag back in place.

"Do you really think I'd believe a lying addict? It's time you pay for the damage you've done to your family."

The boy looks up at me. I walk over to him and cover his eyes with a gloved hand. He doesn't need to see this coming. Poised on the edge of sorrow, I target his heart and press the knife deep into his chest. The blood seeps through his cotton shirt before I start to remove the blade. He twitches as I pull back on the knife like he's come down with a fatal case of hiccups.

I hope with his last thought, he understands this is mercy.

Behind me, I can hear wretched sniveling coming from the mother. She's not crying for the loss of her son. She knows that she's next, and as my time with the son ends, she grows louder and starts edging toward hysterics.

I walk away from the boy without looking at the tiny corpse. His mother is trying to put distance between us by inching herself forward on her stomach. As if she has any chance of escaping her fate. I quickly cross the meager ground between us and jerk her up by the shoulder, flipping her onto her back. I straddle her torso, and she screams in pain from the pressure I'm putting on her arms, now pinned under her back. Leaning on one forearm, placed on the ground next to her head, I parade the knife before her wild stare. Drops of the boy's blood fall thickly onto her cheek. She tries to squirm, but I grip her chin with my free hand and use her face to wipe the blade clean. She's striped with hot tears and her son's blood.

I shift my stance, crouching over her, and stab her under the ribs. She wails with pain. I dangle the bag of drugs in front of her face, open one, and dump it onto the ground. She stretches her eyelids wide over red bleary eyes, displaying more vigor over the wasted drugs than she did while watching her son die. I jab the blade into her again. This time I've buried it up to the hilt in her chest. I leave the knife in place and steadily pour the contents of the last small baggie into one nostril, then the other, a little bit at a time. She tries to lurch away from me but I hold her head in place and wait for her to snort up. With a sharp yank, I reclaim my knife from her chest wound and add several more to the flesh of her stomach while the poison writhes through her circulatory system, highlighting the sharp exchanges between blade and body. It doesn't take much for her to black out with such a high concentration of filth flowing through her veins, and having lost so much blood, it quickly approaches fatal levels.

I sit down, equal parts exhausted and exhilarated.

But I'm not yet done here.

After taking out their gags and loosening the rope, I position the corpses together on one sleeping bag with a second one draped over them like a blanket. I position them so that they appear comfortable and close. He's leaning into her chest with one arm wrapped around him.

I snap a photo—one that shows the only truth the boy ever wanted from her.

The car is no longer visible in the shade of nightfall, but if there's any white residue from the line she snorted earlier, it would make for a nice memento for the investigators who close this area off whenever the bodies are found.

I walk away from the bodies and over to the car, sliding a flashlight out of my bag and clicking it on.

The car comes into view, and I'm amused to see that a thin white smudge remains on the hood. I aim the flashlight down, preparing to stash it in my pocket and free up my hands for the camera, but the light flashes against something on the ground that catches my eye: A photo, crumpled and face down on the dirt. I've never before taken any trophies from a crime scene, but this might be an exception. A photograph for a photograph, and only I would ever know. It's almost too perfect for me to not act on it.

I bend down and turn over the photograph, casting light on an image that sends me to my knees.

There, staring back at me, is Lydia.

Chapter 17

LYDIA

It's been a week since I last saw him. Our dinner date tonight was my idea. Maybe this is what he brings out of me. The more assertive version of myself I've been burying.

It took me a while to reach Adam. When he didn't call me back for two days, I assumed that was the end of it. Those hours spent waiting can ruin anyone.

But, finally, he called me back, apologizing for being such a ghost throughout the week and saying he'd been thinking about me. He caught wind of an estate sale that featured early editions of classic books and immediately drove out of Portland. I didn't want to consider how flimsy the excuse was. So many hours alone in the car, yet he never called me back? I knew my next question would tell me everything I needed to know.

I've never asked anyone out to dinner and felt rather awkward doing it. Adam was obviously taken aback when I asked, covering it up with nervous laughter, but he agreed to it—enthusiastically, even—and we decided on tonight.

I don't want to presume that we'll be coming back to my place, but, just in case, I take down all of the photographs. With each one that I take down, I'm growing more irritated. I had just put them back up after Heather dropped off the map. I thought that she'd get in touch with me before they went to California. I'll be pissed if she left without letting me say goodbye to Jacob. I tried calling her a few times, but her phone went straight to voicemail every time.

The clatter of the door buzzer sets me off like a sprinter. He's here and I'm moving frantically from room to room, making sure all of the forensic photos are down. I really hope I got them all.

I buzz him in and hear a soft knock on my door a few moments later. I take one last look in the mirror. My hair is behaving today. It falls perfectly just beneath my eyebrows. It's the only part of me that I really like because it makes it easy to hide my face from the world.

I run for the door and slow to a walk before I reach it so I don't seem too eager. I swing the door open and he's standing there, wearing black pants and a gray Henley. Standing on the other side of the door frame, I immediately feel overdressed.

"Mind if I change?"

"You look beautiful," he says in a way that I can't read. There's something cold and somber in his voice, something I didn't expect to see when I opened the door.

"Can't I be beautiful and comfy?" I tease.

"Of course you can. I just wanted to compliment you." A smirk rises and drops from his cheek.

"I'm just... not used to compliments. I'll be quick I promise." As I turn, I'm hoping he reaches for me, catching me like he did on the day we first met.

Instead, he says, "Take your time. I'll wait out here."

I leave the door open, but he never comes in.

We decide to make the most of the dry evening and walk to the restaurant instead of taking a cab. It's brisk out, and I'm glad to be in a sweater and out of that dress.

He hasn't said much since we left my apartment. One-word answers and nothing more.

"Did you find any literary treasures?" I try to open him up.

"What?" he responds.

"On your business trip."

"Oh, yeah. Um... Nothing of particular value, no."

"The man who has everything, right?"

He nods. I know his mind is elsewhere.

"Is something wrong?" I ask.

His head flips to me, as if he's been caught. "Why do you say that?"

"You just... don't seem like yourself."

He sighs, slowing his pace until he's at a full stop. I turn to face him, peering up at his bright eyes, which seem to pull in all the lights of the city.

"You're right," he says. "I'm sorry... Listen, I really wanted to take you out tonight, but..."

"If this isn't a good night, we can just do this some other time," I say.

"No, it's not that it isn't a good night. I want to spend time with you, I really do, but I want to be... here. If that makes sense."

It does. He doesn't know me well enough yet to understand how often I get lost in this labyrinthine head of mine. "I get it. Trust me."

He sighs again. "I don't want to sound presumptuous here, but... do you want to come back to my place? We can order takeout, sit around, talk. Read, maybe."

"Are you inviting me to browse your collection of rare books?"

He smiles, and I know he's here now.

Here with me.

We stop in front of a large contemporary house that's set back from the road. Straight edges surround large panes of glass. I'm so embarrassed. Why did I let him see my crappy little studio apartment? It pales in comparison to this.

"Holy shit," I say.

He gives me a confused look and laughs. "What is it?"

"Oh, I just... Nothing."

"Doesn't look like the home of a book dealer and part-time McDowell's employee, does it? I bought the land years ago with some inheritance, and it took me a long time to build this on the lot. I saved my money over the years and did a lot of the work myself. Ultimately, I'm very happy with it. I took the time to make it exactly the way I wanted it. I'm sure you feel the same way about your place."

He's right. My apartment may be tiny, but it's the first place that I have ever been able to call my own. "It's beautiful," I say. "I love how it's set so far back from the street. I'm sure that cuts down on the noise from pedestrians. The walking traffic is so dense around here it's like there's no regard for privacy anymore."

We walk up the paved path to a covered porch. A hammock hangs in one corner, and comfy, oversized patio chairs in another. This porch would be the perfect place to curl up and read during a storm.

"I like living in Portland, but I don't love the population density. I've tried to make this place as private as possible. I've landscaped everything with dense ferns and tall trees lining the property. That way I don't have to see any of my neighbors and can almost feel as if I'm in the wild."

From the porch, I don't see any neighbors, and the sidewalk we just walked up from is buried behind a curtain of wide leaves. It really is an escape from the clamor of the city.

"I feel the same. If I didn't need to be here for my job, I'd be living far out of the city. But then I'd need to have a car. I don't need one with things as they are. I bike to a lot of places. Sometimes I take the bus."

He unlocks the front door and opens it, then flips on a light. I step over the threshold after him and find myself standing on smooth, polished hardwoods, staring into an open space with a living room occupied by upholstered furniture and a dining area with a rectangular oak wood table in the middle of it.

Must've been some inheritance.

His keys *clank* on a small table next to the front door.

"You said you had some family in town, right?" Adam says as he walks through the open floor plan, flipping on more lights and heading into the kitchen.

I close the door and follow him. "Yeah, my sister and her son. Well... I'm technically her *adopted* sister. It's a whole thing."

Without looking back at me he says, "What all have you been up to while they've been in town?" He's obscured by the walls surrounding the frame that leads to the kitchen, but soon reappears and places a bottle of wine on the island. He fastens a corkscrew on top of it.

"What have I been doing with them? Not a whole lot. Last I heard from my sister, she was going to some campsite. I pissed her off, because I always somehow manage to piss her off, and she hasn't answered any of my calls since. I hope she didn't leave without me saying goodbye to my nephew."

He wrestles the cork out of the wine bottle. "Why don't you go take a seat on the couch? I'll bring us some glasses."

Chapter 18

ADAM

With harsh clarity, I remember my first conversation with her; about her frantic search for—Jacob, was it?—all around McDowell's. I never saw her with him though. Had I known sooner, had I seen the photograph before killing them, I don't know if I could have gone through it.

I can't believe the bodies haven't been found yet.

What am I doing? She could get a call any moment that would rip her away from this house. A call that might devastate her. If not because of the sister, then almost certainly because of the child. Did she know of her sister's lies? Her focus on her addiction and her neglect of Jacob? If she did, would she see things my way?

Or would she see a monster?

I join her on the couch, handing her a glass while holding my own. I don't know how this night will end. My pulse bounces in my eardrums, throbbing in a way that makes any fully formed thought impossible.

We touch glasses. I try to make eye contact as we take our first sip, but she avoids my gaze. If I could stare into her eyes, I believe my heartrate might lower just a bit.

I lick red wine off my lips and say, "Something wrong?"

She takes another sip. This time it's longer. A bittersweet breath releases from her mouth. "Talking about my sister, it... It puts me in a bad mood."

"I'm sorry I brought it up."

"No, you were just making conversation. You remembered I had family in town, which was sweet."

"I take it you two weren't close."

"It's a long story."

"Then give me the short version."

She sighs and stares at the red pool swirling in her wine glasses. For a moment, I think she's prepared to consume all of it at once. "Heather's parents—my foster parents—burned to death when we were younger. I bounced back from it better than she did. It was *her* parents, after all. I'm not sure how long she was living on the streets when I reconnected with her, but I helped her get clean. And then she had Jacob. It might be the only good thing she ever did."

No sign of reverence. I'm not sure Heather will be missed. "Is she a good mother to Jacob?" I ask.

Her eyes stab at mine. "She's a terrible mother... Terrible. I don't think she ever stopped using." She rubs her eyes and sniffles.

"It's okay, I'll listen. Or we can just leave it there." I hope she doesn't leave it. I'm yearning for her to validate my kill.

"Some other time, maybe," she says. "Let's talk about something else."

Damn.

"I'm interested to hear more about your job," I say. "You said you're a forensic photographer?"

She leans back against the couch, her face relaxing. "I am. It's been really interesting the past few weeks, actually. I wish I could talk about it, but I'm sworn to secrecy."

"Are you still working on the same case from earlier this week?"

"Yes. Nothing's been released to the press yet, but there are multiple agencies involved in the case. It's something *big*. Like... *really big*. They've excused me from other casework and tasked me to this one exclusively." She's excited, I can tell, but she's making herself hold back. It really does seem like no one's ever understood her fascination with crime. I don't fault anyone for not understanding a person's obsession with the macabre, but that must make her feel as alone as I've felt for so many years.

"I've never had an opportunity like it," she says. "And I've never *seen* anything like it. This killer..."

A knot tightens in my stomach. Is it *me* she's referring to?

She continues. "And I've already said too much... How do you do this to me?" She grins.

My breath shakes as I say, "So there's a killer?"

"I can't say." Her grin becomes a smile.

I take another sip of wine, my hand shaking the glass as I bring it to my lips. "If I were to guess... I'd say you're enjoying taking pictures of his crime scenes."

"Who's to say it's a *he*? Or that there's even a killer at all?" She's toying with me. She wants to talk about the case. "Even if there were... Killing's bad."

"Is it always?" I ask.

Her smile fades. She hesitates to answer. "I don't think so, actually."

"Why do you say that?"

"I think there might be certain circumstances where killing is..." She stops herself.

"Justified?" I finish for her.

Her eyes catch mine, answering in place of words. "Sometimes I think there are some people who just... deserve it. I almost... wish... someone would do something about it. Is that terrible of me to say?"

I want to hold her and tell her it's not terrible at all. I want to tell her what I've done and who I've done it to. I give her a smile. "If that's terrible of you to say, then I'm terrible too. I absolutely agree. Your secret's safe with me."

She smiles back. "Can I tell you a secret?"

"Sure," I say.

She leans in closer. "But you can't tell anybody."

"Of course," I say as her lips brush against mine.

"I hope they don't catch him because this is the most alive I've felt in my entire life."

A steady drip catches my ear. I've tipped over my glass and spilled wine on the carpet.

Lydia laughs. "You need to clean that up?"

"Hell no." I set the glass on the coffee table, grab her shoulders, and pull her body into my embrace, my lips firmly locked on her. Without knowing how it's happened, I'm lying on top of her, kissing her neck. My teeth tug gently at the flesh above her breasts, and she wraps her legs around me, gripping my hair and pulling me in closer.

I take her hands away from my head and with one arm pin them above her.

"Adam, wait..." she says.

I take my lips off her skin.

"I want you... but not like this," she says through quickened breaths.

My breaths come fast as well as I climb off of her and stand by the couch. "Is this all happening too soon?"

She lies on her back, chest rising and falling, rising and falling.

"Can we go upstairs and... just sleep?" she asks.

Chapter 19

LYDIA

He leads me up the stairs.

At the top of the stairs, there are four rooms behind a horseshoe of doors. The doors to two rooms are open. One looks like the bathroom and the other contains large wooden shelving units, lined with hardback books packed together tightly. He glances back at me over his right shoulder and catches me leaning over to see into the room filled with books. I see him catch me and look away casually.

"So the bathroom is obviously there," I point out. "And that room looks like your office or maybe a library. What are the other rooms?" I ask.

"Well, this here is the master bedroom and that one is my home theater. Would you like a tour before we go to bed?"

I walk toward the study and stop before the doorway, so he can lead me in. I'm too damn eager, practically bouncing on the balls of my feet. We enter the room and it's overwhelming. I only recognize a small fraction of the titles that lay before me. But I don't care because I'm in a room filled floor to ceiling with rare books. I'm intoxicated by the smell of the place. Its earthy odor permeates the wood shelves and drifts into the hall. There's something soothing about being surrounded by books, by this much history, some of them are clearly hundreds of years old. It dawns on me that enshrined in this room, a couple meters away from where Adam sleeps, is an incredible amount of history imprinted on paper and bound in leather. We walk to separate areas of the room, and I gingerly handle a few books, inspect their spines, caress the gilded leaves, and then put them back. I steal a glance here and there of Adam, and he of me, but our main focus is the books. Soon I grow tired and all I want to do is lay down on him.

"Can we go to your bedroom? I haven't slept well in days. I'd love to just lie down with you now."

"Of course. Let's go to bed."

His bed sits low and is framed in dark wood. Along the wall behind the bed are matching end tables and a full wall forest mural. On one side of the room, there's a sliding glass door that comprises the whole wall. It looks like it leads to a balcony overlooking the yard. I can see a thick collection of branches swaying in the light of the moon.

"Do you have anything I can sleep in?" I say as he undresses out of sight.

He emerges from his walk-in closet wearing boxer briefs and a white tee shirt with a pair of lounge pants and a black shirt. "I think if you just want to sleep, this will be the safest attire. Although you'll look sexy in that too."

"Oh, hush." I walk into the bathroom and close the door. I change and see myself in the mirror. I don't have my familiar surroundings. The collections of my photographs and the killer's photographs calm me and make me feel safe before bed. Right now, I don't need them. I turn off the bathroom light and open the door. He's already lying in bed. I wonder if that's his side or if he normally sleeps in the middle. When I was growing up, I either had to sleep on the floor or I would be given such a tiny uncomfortable bed that I had to curl up into a ball just to rest. These days, I still only take up a quarter of any real bed, and I haven't slept in a bed with another person for years.

"Do you have a side you like to sleep on?" he says like he's reading my mind.

"No. I have a few cats that are usually asleep before me, they take their pick of bedside and I curl up into a ball in the remaining space."

"Well, before you do that... how about you lie here." He holds out his arm, inviting me to lie on his chest.

I get into bed and move toward him under the covers, laying my head down on his chest as he runs his fingers through my hair.

"Thank you for stopping," I say. "In my experience, not all guys will."

"I've done a lot of things in my life that I'm not proud of, Lydia Walker, but forcing myself on a woman isn't one of them."

I close my eyes, feeling the warmth of his skin on mine.

Sunlight streams through the balcony window. I can't believe that I've slept through the whole night. How long was I out? Adam's side of the bed is empty but warm from the sun that strikes the sheets just below his pillow. The bedroom door hangs open to the hallway.

I walk a few steps to the study and stick my head in. Adam sits at a laptop, behind a giant oak desk surrounded by several books opened to different pages.

He looks at me and perks up immediately. “Good morning. How'd you sleep?

“Better than I have in years, actually. You?”

“I woke up about an hour ago, but that's a lot of sleep for me. I made some coffee, and I can make breakfast if you want.”

“I’m not much of a breakfast person.... But coffee sounds good.”

He closes his laptop. “How do you like your coffee?”

“Half coffee, half milk, and all the sugar.” I laugh.

“So, barely tasting like coffee, but with all the caffeine benefits?”

“Precisely.”

I change back into my clothes from last night and try to check my phone. It’s gone dead. So be it.

I go downstairs to find a black travel mug sitting on the island in the kitchen.

“Is this for me?” I ask him.

“Yes it is,” he responds. “In case you don’t finish, you can take it with you. This way, you have to see me again.” He wraps his arms around my waist and kisses me. “If that’s something you’d be interested in.”

I nestle my face into his chest. It’s so relaxing to rest there, in the same spot where I fell asleep last night.

The reality of my profession threatens to lower me back down to earth.

“Can I borrow a phone charger?” I ask.

“Sure, there’s one over on the counter.” He points to the corner of the kitchen to a charger sitting freely on a marble countertop.

I take a sip of my coffee as I wait for my phone to come back on.

Five missed calls from Frank.

"I'm sorry," I say to Adam. "I have to—"

"No need to apologize. Do what you need to do." He pours coffee into a mug, then leaves the room.

I call Frank and wait for him to answer.

"Finally," he says from the other end. "I've been calling you for hours."

"My phone died. What's going on?"

His voice barely registers a hint of emotion, a cold sting of hopelessness lingering on his tongue. "There's been another double homicide."

Chapter 20

LYDIA

Frank's waiting for me at the front of the station when I arrive. I steady my camera bag against my hip as I walk quickly toward him.

He closes the distance, the worn soles of his dress shoes slapping the pavement as he rushes toward his vehicle.

"It's been about two weeks since the last one, hasn't it?" I say, following him with my eyes, then with my feet. "I was starting to think that he might be working off an established pattern with respect to the time between murders."

"A week passed between the first and second set of victims," Frank says, "but we don't know how long the bodies were sitting there before they were discovered. We'll know soon enough."

I hurry into the car after him. The engine comes to life.

"Where in Portland did he hit this time?" I ask, slipping the seatbelt over my chest.

"It's not in Portland."

"What?"

He begins the slow drive out of the parking lot, picking up speed as he exits. "The victims were found in Washington. Harshaw's got a guy that he's assigned to spend all day listening to different scanner channels and calling stations all through the Pacific Northwest."

"Why Washington..." I say to myself.

"Who the hell knows? There's going to be a mess of uniforms there this morning. Washington State Police, Portland Police Bureau, FBI, and the local sheriff will be there, along with some I'm sure I've missed. We weren't necessarily called in on this one, but a strongly worded request was sent out. We should definitely be present when they first go through the crime scene."

"But... What makes them so sure it's our guy? He's never crossed state lines before."

"I don't know how convinced they are, but, speaking for me... Remote campsite. A rental car found near the area. Apparently, the bodies were staged. Pretty cut and dry."

"Do we know anything else about the victims?"

"They were discovered only a few hours ago by a man hunting nearby, but that's all we've got. We'll need to tread lightly on this one. You should know that it's because of you that we're involved in the first place. We used your portfolio to convince them we should be there."

"Me... How?"

"Their usual forensic photographer is on vacation in Hawaii. We told them you've been on the case from the beginning, and since there are similarities with the ones we've already seen, it would be vital to have you go over it."

"God forbid Washington Police get involved and solve the case before Portland Public Bureau or the FBI does."

"If anyone solves this case, I'd have my money on you." He turns to me without a smile or nod, catching my eyes for a second before turning back to the road ahead.

My heart leaps as I consider it might be a look of respect.

"I know this stuff revs your engine," he says. "You seem more interested in this case than any other one I can remember you working on. I may not get it, but... you're closer to thinking like this damn lunatic than I could ever attempt to. I've been treating that like a bad thing. Anything you have to say about this case, you let it rip—You hear me? Don't hold back just because this grumpy old man doesn't want to hear it."

I crack a sly smile. "You need me."

"Come on, don't push it... But, yes, I do."

A joyful warmth consumes me, relaxing my back against the passenger's seat. "Thank you for saying that, Frank."

"What's with you goin' dark on me all morning?" Frank says.

"I told you. My phone went dead."

"That's not like you. If I had to guess..."

I chuckle. "Maybe it's best you don't guess."

Police cruisers clutter the roadside, leading to a dirt entrance blocked by a single uniformed officer. Frank holds his badge out the window, and the officer steps aside.

"With this being outside our jurisdiction," Frank tells me, "we *need* to verify that it's the same killer. We'll have a chance at providing vital information. Washington will have to let us on the case. If they won't, who's to say an official from Portland wouldn't leak information to the press?"

"Aren't you surprised that it hasn't leaked yet?"

Frank parks in a dirt lot swarming with marked cars and SUVs. "I think the fear is that our resources will be put to waste if we have to follow up with every tip that comes in. We'd be bogged down by callers just looking for the reward, instead of anyone actually providing useful information. We really don't have much to tell the press either. If this were an abduction case, it would be a completely different story. But we can keep the perp guessing by being silent. If we were to go to the press, he'd be a lot better educated on how close we're getting, or not getting."

With that, he gets out of the car and walks over to a cluster of detectives and local police. Frank is all smiles. He shakes hands all around and even spares a hug for one guy. For a grumpy old cop, he sure is popular. I stay in the car a few more minutes to go over my gear, prep the camera, take test shots, and check settings. I'm sure I'll have to tweak things some more, considering that the campsite is hidden from the road and the sunlight is closed off by a dense tree cover.

The parking lot is filled with men and women clad in various shades of blues and browns, wielding badges from Washington and Oregon. At the edge of the parking lot, as I'm about to enter the path to the campsite, an officious arm stretches out in front of me blocking my path. I'm nearly clotheslined.

"Just where in the hell do you think you're going? How did you even find out we were out here?" he demands.

I turned to Frank, who's already on his way over. "There a problem?" he hollers.

"Can you believe the tenacity of these press people? They'll do anything for a goddamn story."

At this, Frank can't defuse his chuckles.

"What could possibly be funny about this?" he scolds.

"Detective Bryan Conners, please meet Lydia Walker," Frank says, "Portland Police Bureau's in-house forensic photographer."

Conners swings his gaze back at me.

"At your service, Detective," I sneer.

Conners' face flushes bright red with embarrassment. He fights to compose himself. He doesn't apologize, just takes a step back. A ruckus of jokes and snickers bubbles from a huddle of officers nearby. I'm not surprised. Most men can't recognize authority or skill from an unexpected direction. On top of that, this one's a detective. In the past few years, I've worked with plenty of cops and detectives. A majority of them are good at their jobs, but stubborn and hot-headed.

"Miss Walker, thank you for coming out," Conners says.

"Not a problem. Could you lead the way, Detective? I wouldn't want to go anywhere I'm not supposed to."

Frank lets out a low rumbling chuckle as I pass. We follow Detective Conners down a narrow path that leads from the nearby one-lane highway into the dense woods. The area is so deserted that I haven't heard more than two trucks since our arrival ten minutes ago. The path terminates in a small clearing up ahead, but I can't see much of anything past Conners.

I hear the crunching of fall leaves below my feet and can't help but smile. It's only September, but some trees have already reached their seasonal peak and begun the descent into hibernation.

We follow Conners into a low clearing. Without turning, he says,

"Brace yourselves."

I edge closer to the crime scene, an otherwise serene location now littered with officials, murmuring to each other, scampering around slowly.

And I see the two of them.

I drop to my knees.

The scene in front of me is a blur from the tears in my eyes as I stare straight at them. Heather and Jacob are in front of me, lying in each other's arms, dead and badly decomposed. They were found much later than the other victims. I close my eyes tight, but I can still see Jacob's flesh, half-rotted and churning with maggots, behind the book propped in Heather's lap. Before I have time to process this scene any further, Frank is kneeling down with his arm around me. I look at him blankly. His mouth is moving but I can't understand what he's saying to me. It's like I'm underwater and everything I see and hear is distorted. I draw myself up and use every ounce of concentration I have to make out what he's saying.

"Lydia! Lydia! What's wrong?! Can you hear me? Goddammit, say something."

"Heather and Jacob," I whisper. My body feels heavy on the ground. I lift my arm and point a finger at them.

"What? Do you know them?" Frank says.

I try to speak, but all I can muster are short breaths. I could fall apart here and now, letting the pieces of my body sink into the soil that's been tainted with Jacob's blood. I warned Heather, didn't I? She didn't listen. Could I have tried harder? Could I have done anything to keep Jacob safe?

"Let's get you out of here," Frank says. "You don't need to see this."

Frank lifts me, groaning as his body hinges upright. I can hardly feel my legs under me. The universe has deemed it fit to challenge my own twisted views on justice. Someone or something out there heard my pleas. Somehow, someone knew that my sister was a life-long liar, consumed by selfish desires, that I wish she'd died in that fire with her parents.

Somehow, the killer knew Jacob would always live a life of torment.

It's as if I myself had committed the act.

The last horrible reminder of my past is finally gone, the pieces of me I couldn't remove before, buried in that dirt.

I have to go back and see this through.

We're almost out of the clearing when I stop. "Wait..."

Frank's grip eases on my arms. "We need to get you back to the car."

I wipe my tears. "It's my sister and nephew. Heather and Jacob."

"Jesus, Lydia..."

"They were visiting from Northern California. She lived here for a long time but she's just a tourist like the others... *Was* a tourist."

"Lydia, we really don't have to do this right now."

"I'm okay. I can still do this."

"If, at any time, I don't think you can handle it, you're off the case. No arguments. Understood?" I don't think Frank has ever spoken to me so sternly in the whole time I've known him. At this moment he almost feels like my father.

"I understand... I have to photograph the scene."

Eventually, he'll ask me why I think she was targeted—I know he will. Any good investigator would. But I can't have Frank or anyone else digging around in my head. The last remnants of my past are dead. They lie a few feet from where I stand.

I loved Jacob, even though I always hated the name Heather gave him. Thinking his name makes me feel sick. It's not his fault that every time I heard the name, I would think of his grandfather. Heather couldn't begin to imagine why that would be a problem. How would she have known? I never told her that her beloved daddy would make me say his name while he forced himself in me.

In spite of the boy's innocence, he was another reminder.

I need the photos... I need them to be mine. Later tonight, I'll be hanging them on the walls in my bedroom. I'll lie down on my bed, and as I scan the deadly collage, I'll expose myself to all the emotions that I've bottled up during the years since Heather's father's death.

I know that later I'll be surrounded by images of the dead, I only need to tolerate the living for a while longer today. Frank and I walk back to the campsite so I can return to my work.

I begin by taking a few shots of the entire scene through my wide-angle lens. Some of the shots I take are easier to digest than others since the killer has propped them in such a way that a book blocks Jacob's face.

When I move closer, I see maggots in Heather's sunken eyes. I think back to a class I recently taught, subbing for an out-of-town professor, about decomposition and what to expect. Flies land on recently dead flesh and lay eggs. When those eggs hatch they become disgusting maggots. They feed on the rotting flesh until they've undergone enough growth to metamorphose into flies, who land and lay eggs again. Over and over again these wriggling agents of decay conduct their cycle until nothing is left. By the state of Heather and Jacob, I'd say they've already been fed on a few times.

Heather's eyes are missing and the lids that once shielded the globes have been torn back like undue window dressing. Her mouth is ajar, and the maggots have taken to it gleefully, just another orifice to conquer. It appears that here, like in the other scenes, the killer took the time to position them together. But after so much time has passed it's impossible to see the intended scene. Their remains cuddle around a book. Jacob's head teeters on her shoulder but one arm has flopped down and his knuckles drag on the ground. It's as if we're the audience at a show of defunct marionettes, their puppet master long gone, and the strings tangled from disuse. The show stars one dead drug addict and a poor little boy. In my head, this commentary plays in a loud, animated voice like a game show announcer.

What the fuck is wrong with me?

I move my lens down toward the ground and focus on a pile of photos through the tiny viewfinder. I drop the camera and let it bob on the strap around my neck. Moving closer, I focus in on one single photo. I have to see it with my own eyes. Through the imposed perspective of the killer, through his eyes I see the lies and the truth in the photographs he's left behind. Heather treated him like he was a nuisance. Like a piece of garbage—the way I was treated all through my childhood.

I'm glad the bitch is dead. I don't need remorse for her.

I stand above Heather's corpse, clenching my fists so hard that my fingernails tear pieces of skin off my palms. I want to smash in what's left of her face with my boot. I want to ground her into the wet earth next to the powdered plastic bag beside her chair. Was she getting high on their camping trip? The goddamned nerve it takes to be so self-centered.

In one photograph, Jacob and Heather are covered in blood and look as if they're frozen in time. It was taken before the onset of decay. Before they turned into the rotting corpses I saw in front of me, devoured by the insects and the elements.

Frank's worried gaze moves from the road to me and back to the road, a cadence that repeats itself all the way back to the station. I think that there are some days, more than others, where I remind him of his daughter. If she was alive, she'd be around my age. Frank and his wife could never bring themselves to have another child after her murder.

His jaw goes limp. "I'm sorry about your sister and the kid... I realize I haven't said that yet."

"Thank you. I didn't realize she was still on drugs. She must have been a good fit for this guy. She was just like the other victims."

"You don't know that for sure."

"No... but it's perfectly likely."

"Are you sure you want to go to the station? I can take your camera and one of the forensic photo technicians can make prints of your digital images for the team. "

"No. I want to do it myself," I say without hesitation.

"I just figured you'd want to go home. I know I would."

"You know how particular I am about my pictures."

"Okay, but I'm keeping my eye on you, and as soon as you're done, I want you at home tonight and tomorrow."

"Unless more bodies are found."

"Not even then. We'll have to bring in someone else."

"Frank, I'm fine. I'll take tonight and tomorrow, but don't take me off this case. You said as long as you could keep an eye on me, you'd keep me on."

"The thing is, I don't know if we *can* keep you on. You know in a few days we'll have to bring you into the station."

"Why?"

"For one thing, you were probably one of the last people to see your sister alive. Secondly, you're the only local to have lost a loved one. We're going to need your angle on her and why she was targeted. And third, you've been to each crime scene. The victims of the other families aren't here, and they can't have any idea what we're up against."

"I'll come in, but I'm not sure how much help I can be." I'm already dreading it. I'm able to omit things when it suits me, but when I'm directly asked a question, I'm a horrible liar.

"Maybe tomorrow or the next day, as soon as you're up for it. Of course, the sooner you get in the better for everyone involved."

I don't respond. I close my eyes and all I see is fire. I can't tell them. I won't. I'm not sure at that moment what I'm going to say.

Truth be told, I fit this killer's pattern as much as Heather does. My only saving grace is that I tailor my truths better than Heather did. If Frank knew, he wouldn't forgive me for what I've done. All I want to do is to go home and process this fucked up day.

Chapter 21

ADAM

Lydia had said that she'd call after work, but she hasn't yet. She left in a hurry this morning, apologizing as she did, with my travel mug in her hand. One rushed kiss and she was out the door.

I think they found the bodies today. If they did, what does that mean for her and me?

I hope they don't catch him because this is the most alive I've felt in my entire life. Her whisper repeats in my head, over and over. At that moment I was released from my fear. It gave me hope. She wants to understand the killer. To understand me.

I watched her sleeping in my arms last and composed a mental collage of the various features of her face. Her soft olive-colored skin scattered with moles and birthmarks. I ran my fingers through her black hair, releasing the messy bun from on top of her head and wrapping the loose strands that framed her face around my fingertips. Lydia stirred a few times in her sleep and eventually pulled her knees to her chest. She squirmed her way to one of the corners of the bed just like she had described. But in my bed, she woke up to the light, not shrouded in darkness. It was a new day. Everything had changed.

Even though I didn't sleep in quite as late as Lydia, I slept later than I have in years. There have been so many mornings where I wake up in abject fuzziness, feeling like I've forgotten all the aspects of my life. After a few moments, I'm caught up on all the intricate details. It's fairly disappointing, and I've begun to dread mornings and that associated feeling. Today I welcomed it. I woke up with my head turned to the balcony door looking at the world beyond.

I need to call her.

I listen to long, drawn-out rings on the other end and a split second of silence before I'm prompted to leave a voicemail. She doesn't have a personalized message. I guess she never bothered to set it up, so I'm left with the automated one. I call only once and leave one message. I don't want to seem pathetic or too eager. Maybe I only imagined that we had shared such a rich connection.

I'm standing in my study looking down at the photo of her staring back at me, the same photo I took from the crime scene. Since her departure yesterday morning, I've come in here and opened this book—the book I selected to hide the photo in—a dozen times. I remember how my body tensed as I watched Lydia glide her hand along the spines of my collection before we went to bed. She could have so easily discovered it then, right there in front of me, but I didn't stop her. Maybe I wanted her to find it—if only to remove that one barrier she didn't know existed between us.

If the bodies have been discovered, if Lydia rejects me for the monster others would assume I am, the photo will be a reminder of how I lost her.

My phone vibrates against the oak wood desk. I hit answer before I look to see who it is. It's got to be after midnight, considering I can only faintly hear the street through the open balcony door.

"Hello?" she says.

"Lydia?" I grumble, trying hard to remove the sleep from my voice.

"Yeah, it's me. Look I'm sorry to call so late, but... I need to see you." She sounds upset, like she's been crying.

They found them.

"Do you want me to come over?" The line almost sounds like it's gone dead. I can't hear anything but the hiss of the line, and the rushing blood in my ears.

"I'd rather come over there, if that's okay?"

"Sure, I'm here. Come over."

"I'm on my way." She hangs up before I can respond.

My watch reads 12:18 a.m. I don't know if she's walking or driving, so I can't estimate when she'll be here. I draw the blinds for the bay window in the living room and sit down in the chair next to the fireplace. From here, I'll be able to see her walking up the path to my front door.

I sit, watch, and wait.

I see her shadow on the sidewalk obscured by rainfall as she hurries to the front door and knocks quietly but urgently. When I swing open the door, she's soaked head to toe and shaking. She stands there looking at me in a shell-shocked state, dripping wet and holding herself tightly.

She walks past me into the living room and sits on the couch, staring into the flames. I sit down next to her and wait for her to say something.

"You know that case I've been working on?"

"I remember you mentioning a little about it."

"Well... earlier today we surveyed another crime scene and the victims were... I knew them."

"Holy shit." I feel guilty feigning ignorance, but I have to. Maybe if I'm able to read her better, after tonight, I might risk telling her the truth. It would be worth it to walk through this life with someone I trust, who truly understands me.

"It was my foster sister and nephew. The killer—" She hesitates.

I know she wants to tell me, but part of her doesn't want to say too much. I put her hand in mine and kiss her cheek, and then I pull away, looking at her gently. I'll wait all night if I have to for her to open up to me.

"I shouldn't be telling you this. Case details are strictly confidential, and to breach security like this is a fireable offense, but I need to tell someone, and for some crazy reason, I want to tell you." She looks at me and I can see the tension drain from her shoulders and chest as she makes up her mind.

"Fuck it," she says. "If I don't give you any specific crime scene details, I'm not technically breaking protocol. Here goes. There's a killer. There are now three sets of victims. In each occurrence, he targeted multiple related victims at remote camping sites. He seems to be targeting tourists and particularly those people that have been lying to the ones they love."

I already know all of this, Lydia. If only I could tell you, we'd save a lot of time.

She gets up off the couch and starts to pace back and forth in a manic state.

"I've been home for the past few hours looking through the photos from the crime scene and the thing is... I'm not sorry she's dead. The killer revealed the truth to me. She would always be a drug addict. And the way she treated Jacob... I miss him. I really do... But he's better off."

It takes every bit of composure I have to stop myself from kissing her at that moment. She understands me. I stand up and block her so she'll stop pacing.

"You feel guilty because in a way you're relieved," I say.

Tears fill her eyes, and she nods. There's something else she's holding back. I squeeze her tight, nestling my head down into her neck.

"You have no reason to feel guilty. She's the liar, the drug addict, the horrible parent, not you," I assure her.

"I thought you'd think I was fucked up because I felt relieved and not devastated."

"I don't think there's anything wrong with you for how you feel."

She kisses me, tenderly at first, and then all at once, her embrace is full of passion. I hoist her body onto mine and she wraps her legs around me and grabs my hair. I suddenly need to have every part of her body close to mine. I hold her up with my hands cupped under her. Still wrapped in her wet clothes and gripping my torso with pulsing, writhing legs, I lean her against the wall in the living room and we continue to kiss. I take one hand off of her ass to unbutton the black blouse and she doesn't stop me. She arches her back so her exposed bra presses against my chin. I kiss up her neck and along her chest as I expose her breasts, sliding her bra strap down over her shoulder and onto one side.

I stop for a moment and lower her to the ground on bare feet. "Are you sure?"

"Yes," she whispers.

I take her hand and lead her upstairs.

In the bedroom, we undress in front of each other and get into bed. For a while, we lie still, holding each other. Caresses become kisses, and then we move together, making love.

I've never liked that phrase "making love", but I believe in it now.

We fall asleep, intertwined in each other's arms as the sun rises.

Chapter 22

LYDIA

I don't think I've ever been this happy in my life. It's terrifying.

I was sitting at home last night looking at the photos I'd taken before I decided to call Adam. I was surrounded by images of Heather and Jacob, and those of the scene itself. I was scolding myself for the relief I felt, leading to more guilt.

I've tried so hard to only let people in slowly, but most of the time they're so abrasive and prone to rush things. I've come off harsh and standoffish, but I'm neither. I've just needed time. After so many failed attempts at dating, I've become cynical, but with Adam, I think my hope has been renewed.

I let the sunshine warm my face. The rest of me is buried under a mountain of blankets. I've always adored sleeping like this, burrowing deep into a mound of covers, with only my face exposed. It makes me feel safe. I think about last night and replay my personal reel of sexy memories. These will forever be imprinted in my mind.

Adam isn't next to me. The scent of coffee wafts into the room. I crawl over to his side of the bed since it's warmer than mine. As I lay my head down on his pillow, I close my eyes.

I could get used to this.

I venture into his study, viewing his collection of books on floor-to-ceiling shelves. Sturdy hardbacks with embossed spines fit together like pieces of a tapestry. I hover my finger over the rows, careful not to touch them—a rare book dealer likely has rules regarding classic book handling—taking in the comforting aroma of weathered pages.

Until one hardcover with no lettering catches my eye. The white corner of something thin and sharp, sandwiched between the pages, peaks. As I look closer, an edge of exposed film reveals itself to me.

A photograph.

The sight triggers a cavalcade of photographs dancing in my mind. Those of Heather and Jacob joined by those of the other victims as well.

I shake my head, commanding myself to rattle the images free. Not here. Not while I'm with Adam.

Curiosity guides my hand to the spine of the book, its rough texture rubbing against my fingertips, so worn I feel it might crumble in my grip.

I splay the book open.

And I'm looking at a photo of myself staring back at me.

Staring back at Jacob holding his small instant camera on the crowded Portland streets.

The book shakes in my hands as they tremble.

It was Adam.

He killed them all.

I can't breathe. My thoughts cascade around me and I don't know what any of it means. I don't know how to feel or what to do. Does he know my connection to Heather and Jacob? Did he realize when I was sobbing last night that the very people I was crying for were the ones he killed?

Did I lead him to Heather and Jacob?

I slap the book shut, wedging Jacob's photograph within the pages again, and place it back in its spot.

I rush into the hallway, then into Adam's bedroom, searching for clothes.

My bag and keys are downstairs. I have to say something to him before I leave. If I don't, he may suspect something. I don't know if I'll be able to keep everything straight.

I head down the stairs and grab my purse from the living room, then stick my head in the kitchen. He looks up and frowns once he sees that I'm all dressed and ready to go out the door.

"You're doing this again?" he says playfully through the layer of hurt.

"I'm sorry, but... I need to go." I begin to turn away.

He grabs my hand in a way that's quickly becoming familiar, a way that's still comforting despite what I know. I should be recoiling at his touch, hearing sirens blasting in my ears, warning me of the threat he imposes. I know all of this, and yet my body welcomes his touch.

Once again, I'm forced to wonder just what the fuck is wrong with me.

"I want to give you something before you go."

He walks across the kitchen and out of view, raising his voice. "After the first night you came over, I wanted to give you something. I was inspired by our night together." He returns with his hands behind his back. "I saw this and thought of you. I really hope you like it."

From behind his back, he removes a small, square box about the size of an instant photograph. My mind returns to Jacob's photo of me upstairs, now a permanent fixture in his collection.

"You... didn't have to get me anything." I have to keep my hands steady and my breathing slow. He'll see through my attempts to act surprised.

I take off the lid and coil on the downy stuffing. In the center of the box is one of the most beautiful and intricate necklaces I've ever seen. I put it up to the light in my hand with great care. Its silver chain spreads from a pendant of wood and glass. A Death's Head Hawkmoth is encased within, strung up by its wings. It's a symbol only someone like me would understand. Someone who's cherished the words of *The Silence of the Lambs* for so many years.

Without saying a word, he takes it from my hand and steps behind me. The necklace floats through the air in front of me and the wooden moth lands on my chest. I gather my hair up into my right hand and hold it to expose my neck.

He could strangle me so easily now. But somehow, I know he won't.

Adam closes the clasp of the necklace, and my skin rises with goosebumps at the light graze of his hands. I brush the details of the pendant under my thumb and fingers. It's delicate and nearly weightless around my neck.

His breath catches my neck. "I think it captures our shared passion for the darker side of things."

"I love it," I say, thumbing the smooth texture atop my chest.

He's right, of course, but part of me doesn't want him to be. Not now. I think maybe if I walk out of this house right now, I can try to forget the time I've spent with him and what I know. Then I look at him. I'm clearly kidding myself.

Finally, I turn to him. "I wish I could stay, but..." The reason doesn't come. The truth is screaming from behind my lips and beneath my throat—a truth that I can't reveal.

I put the jewelry box in my purse, pull the strap over my shoulder, and I walk out of his door. He doesn't grab me this time.

The morning is brisk, causing me to hug myself for warmth as I try to settle my nerves. Early morning in Portland is the best time to walk the city. Portland is beautiful before it fills up with distractions. Before bikers, children, dog walkers, and smokers start loitering around the neighborhoods. Before the homeless start digging through the recycling bins. The temporarily quiet streets allow my thoughts to settle. I'm unsure if I can ever bring myself to see this man again.

What kind of person does it make me if I fall in love with a serial killer? What kind of person stays, knowing the truth?

Chapter 23

ADAM

I've had a week of silence from Lydia. My mind tricks me into thinking I've seen her everywhere I go. Yesterday, I thought she was crossing a busy city street with her nose in a book. Today there's a girl at the corner table in McDowell's cafe behind stacks of true crime books.

I don't want to be here today, shelving books in the horror section, but I've needed to get out of the house this week. This is where my trouble began, out with the masses and overhearing their lies. I was sick of standing by and letting people treat each other like shit. I chose instead to put them out of their misery.

It's always amusing how openly people will talk about their personal and professional lives in an aisle at a bookstore. You give a person the illusion of isolation and they take on the role of the penitent in a confessional. You never know who could be listening on all sides from other aisles, but that doesn't stop some people from broadcasting their life story. It's usually minor things: a woman saying she drove away from a fender bender and felt awful, a mother confessing to giving her daughter a little Benadryl because she wanted the girl to sleep through the night. These aren't the moral pillars of the community, but they aren't quite trash either.

I shelve the last cart of my shift and look forward to the silence that awaits me back home. It's been weeks since I last killed, and part of me is aching for the next. I haven't brought myself to do it again. Maybe it's because of Lydia, and maybe I just haven't run into the right victims. I'm sick of wasting so much of my day leading them out into the middle of nowhere. It gives me much more time with them before they're found, and I don't have to haul them anywhere, but I'm feeling the urge to kill. There are just so many liars out there who not only deserve to die but also need to die.

I *need* to kill them.

I think about it all the way home and I pass a couple whose lives I could quickly end with my blade. If I killed in the city, it would open me up to many opportunities for watching potential victims. I could make certain that they were as immoral as they seemed. If there was a one-time slip or someone maybe didn't fit the overall type, then I'd give them a second chance. Of course, the forest offered intimacy and privacy but if I make the city work for me there could be many benefits to offset the additional challenges. After all, I have gotten better, more organized.

At home, I light a fire and sit over a legal pad, drumming my pen on the coffee table. The reflection flickers faintly in the darkened room. I've already murdered eight people and there's been no knock at my door. If there was, what then?

But I've left no clues. I've been careful, haven't I?

With Lydia having gone silent, my paranoia that she suspects me grows. If they somehow discovered it was me, the knowledge would have to have come from her.

I need a distraction.

I make a list of all the things I'll need when I decide to kill. Likely, I'll find a victim in the street, though it could be in a hotel or even in their own home. The last option is my favorite, and it would give me the opportunity to take photographs of the scene and spend plenty of time with the victims. I don't want to give up that part of the experience if I decide to move forward with this. It will have to be a place where I can watch unnoticed for quite a while. I think I'll take a stroll through some neighborhoods tomorrow to see what opportunities present themselves. I'm still going to be very particular about my quarry but this way I'll have a large variety to choose from. Of course, I'll need to set myself up in Seattle and rent a hotel room for a couple nights. Use my credit card there and support some local businesses. I'll head up the I-5 in the afternoon and then take the coast all the way back. I'll stop at a few places along the way home and cross items off this shopping list.

Chapter 24

LYDIA

My reflection taunts me in the two-way mirror.

I'm at the station inside of the interrogation room. The lights are harsh fluorescents, and other than the heavy steel table that I'm leaning against, the only other pieces of furniture in the room are two empty chairs. At the lobby desk, I let the duty officer know I was here for an appointment, and instead of having me wait there with him, he led me in here as if I'm under suspicion.

Why would I have to be interviewed here? I'm not a suspect.

Shit...

Actually, now I'm an accessory after the fact, considering the information I've been sitting on the information for almost a week now.

I've spent the last week at home in between my early morning and late-night walks through the city. I mostly walk around my apartment like it's a museum, occasionally stopping to appreciate the art around me. I look at my photographs of his handiwork, remembering back to the second crime scene, remembering me standing where he stood, feeling the power and the perspective of that moment. I think about the courage it takes to do what he's done, and also about the madness that has to be consuming him.

I've taken that time to consider whether there's a similar madness in me too.

Agent Harshaw enters the room with Frank in tow, and the two men stand across from me, each holding a Styrofoam cup filled with stale coffee. Harshaw has a case file tucked under his right arm. The dull chairs make a nasty screeching sound when they're dragged over the concrete floor, worse than nails on a chalkboard, and I try not to visibly cringe.

Harshaw speaks first. "Having you at the scene of a relative of yours was completely out of the norm, but I am glad that you stuck it out and did the photography."

I'm not sure if he's expecting a response to this compliment, but he's not getting one. I cross my arms and lean back in the metal chair.

"I wanted you to come down here so we could talk to you about your sister and your nephew," he adds.

"My *foster* sister," I correct him.

"That's why we couldn't find much on you. I had been looking under Lydia Carlson."

"So you ran a background check on me?"

"We did a general check when you first started working at the PPB. Though now, with the gravity of the case you're on—one that involves multiple agencies—we've gone ahead with a much more in-depth profile on you."

"This is beginning to feel like I'm a person of interest."

"Lydia..." Frank says. "You know how this works. It's just a formality. Please be cooperative."

I readjust myself, lifting one leg over the other. "Carlson is Heather's last name. I never took it. I bounced around foster homes so much that I honestly had forgotten what my birth name was. Once I aged out of the system, I got to pick a new name for a fresh start."

"When did you last see Heather?" Harshaw asks, trying to rattle me.

I need to make a decision. If I tell them about McDowell's, it could lead them to Adam. I don't want him getting caught. Not yet.

"I don't remember what day it was, but I got lunch at the food trucks downtown. I remember her saying that she and Jacob had been all around the city that day window-shopping and that they planned to hit a couple restaurants later on."

"And that was the last time you saw her?"

"Yes. I was going to spend more time with them, but I got called into work for an emergency briefing by Agent Yates. If I'm not mistaken, it may have been the day he arrived in Portland."

Agent Harshaw looks down at the case file and then up at me with a confused look on his face. "That was last week."

"That sounds right."

"And you didn't report her missing after you hadn't heard from her in a few days when you knew she was visiting the area?"

"We didn't have the best relationship," I offer with fake sincerity. "Ignoring me for days at a time is... *was*... normal."

Agent Harshaw leans in sympathetically, and I know I've hooked him. The dead can't talk, so here's my time to embellish a bit.

"She was like a sister to me for a few years. That was... until her parents—my foster parents—died tragically in a house fire." I turn away, feigning a wistful look.

"So you two were the only survivors?"

In that house, I survived more than he could ever imagine. "We were very lucky we got out."

In reality, Heather never got out because she was never in the burning house. She was supposed to be, but she was prone to sleepwalking. That night I found her outside, I could see her in the distance sitting on the wet grass in her purple nightgown with a ratty doll in one hand. I had thought she was inside, but since she wasn't, I simply took her by the wrists and dragged her across the lawn so she'd sit near me by the front door. I remember kneeling there on the ground and looking up at the house. We could hear a faint coughing just under the roar of the flames and I remember praying that *he* wouldn't come running out.

"You mean you were lucky you weren't in the fire," Harshaw says.

I try not to think about that long night and the early morning that followed. The fire made it impossible to tell when the dawn actually arrived. The sunrise was painted over by the waves of purple smoke, the bright glow of flames in front of us. Fourteen years old and I was finally free of him. Free of *them*—that whole damn deceitful family.

Regardless of the sick feeling the act had lodged permanently in my stomach, I've held out hope that I could live on knowing I had done what was necessary.

While knowing that I'm a monster.

I can channel these emotions I've bottled up in the intervening years to put on a show for these two. I need to pull myself back to that time before the fire. The reaction won't play otherwise. So I hug my body and force my eyes down, digging my nails into my skin so hard that it brings tears to my eyes. The thoughts come unrestrained. All of the pain and suffering Heather's father put me through seeps through my eyes, streaming down my face.

Frank rushes over to my side of the table and tries to comfort me.

"Lydia, I didn't mean to upset you," Harshaw says. "I was just trying to gather information." He pauses. "Did you know she was doing drugs?"

Frank whips his head to Harshaw. "I think that's enough for today, don't you?"

I take a few deep breaths and give Harshaw a quick nod. I know I'm in the clear now. For all he knows, I'm sobbing for my dead sister.

"It's okay, Frank," I say. "I can stay. I just want this to be over with so I can move on."

Frank exhales. "Okay." He makes his way back to his seat.

He's skeptical. That's good for me.

I square myself up, wipe my eyes, and answer Harshaw's question. "I didn't know about her current usage. She used to be an addict before Jacob was born. She wasn't picky. Meth, coke, heroin... Whatever it was, it cost her a lot. When we crossed paths, she was in a bad way, digging out of trash cans and living on the street, still doped up and pregnant. I helped her to get clean and I thought that she'd been clean since. She left Portland pretty soon after getting out of rehab to go live in Northern California, trying to avoid the old triggers and bad influences."

"Do you know where exactly she moved to?"

"The last I knew it was Redding. I would send Jacob letters from time to time, but never to Heather, and she detested the phone. I can find the address and give it to you. Last week was the first time I'd seen either of them in person in over five years. I'm sorry... I really can't help you because I didn't know her very well."

Harshaw takes on a formal tone. "Every piece of information you've given us will be useful. In a case like this, anything can prove to be the insight that makes the difference. I appreciate you taking the time." He shuts the folder in front of him.

"Thank you. I hope I was at least able to flesh out some personal details for you." I get up from my chair and pick it up instead of pushing it in, being careful not to evoke that hellacious sound of metal on concrete. When I bend to pick up my purse off the ground, Adam's necklace nearly slips out of my shirt. I place a hand on my chest before it does.

"You were very helpful," Harshaw says. "I'm sure much of that was painful to talk about."

"It's fine. I don't talk about it much. I've never wanted or needed sympathy. I want to come in and do my job and be respected for that, not treated differently. That being said..."

Frank jumps in. "We'll keep the details on a need-to-know basis. Anyone at the Bureau who doesn't need to know... won't." He looks at Harshaw for confirmation.

Harshaw nods.

I walk out the door quickly, speeding down the hall and past the front desk. I just want to get outside and breathe.

I know there's only one person with whom I can truly rehash my past. I'll tell him all about the fire and the abuse because I know his secrets. We have nothing to lose but each other.

Recollecting the morning of the fire brought me to understand how alike Adam and I are. I need to tell him everything.

It's been a week since I last spoke with Adam—since I discovered his secret. I find myself wondering how he's been filling those days.

Chapter 25

ADAM

I look back at myself in the mirror at the local gym, pleased as I ball my gym clothes up and stuff them in a paper grocery bag to burn later. I step into the public shower and scrub myself head to toe just as I did at the beginning of the night. I go back through the past few days. Every second of the hunt felt good. I feel more confident about this murder than any of the ones before. It was easier than I had thought it would be.

I was out walking around town earlier this week, scoping out different neighborhoods. I walk during the day, so as not to seem suspicious with my telephoto lens and camera dangling from my neck. I found that several different areas of the city allow me to gain high ground and peer into the lives of the folks below. I mapped out all traffic cameras and the different storefronts equipped with CCTV. It's the beginning of fall, so

I don't look abnormal wearing a loose hoodie and a large hat.

Along one classy lane, I distinctly heard the squeal of a dog—not a howl or a frightened bark, but a cry of peril—followed by the calls of several other dogs. I walked up to the house but couldn't see into the overgrown backyard. With its years-old paint peeling off of the siding, the place looked quite unappealing, especially considering that all of the neighboring houses were newer and I could tell that their owners took beautiful care of them. The road was defined by luscious gardens and professional landscaping, and a child's bike was left on one lawn. Each house had a porch with a swing or chairs and hanging plants. Not this derelict.

I circled the block, and when I returned a grotesquely overweight man was dragging a black trash bag that left a streak of red on the sidewalk. I didn't want to consider what was in the bag, but I knew it was heavy and filled the entirety of the thin plastic. Every step he took was accentuated by grunts of exhaustion. He stuffed it in the trunk of his car, groaning at the smudge of blood on one of his hands, and drove off.

What a disgusting waste of a human being he was. To kill an innocent animal and treat the disposal as a burden. I decided to tentatively devote my day to watching him. A day in the life of the foul animal killer.

I was able to see his house and into the backyard from the top of a nearby parking garage. Luckily, my perch also faced Mt. Hood, so I ended up looking like a photographer out to get city shots with the mountain view as the backdrop.

It took him until afternoon to reappear. He circled around to the back door and let his dogs out—a dozen total, from what I could see. He entered his home and came back out with a plate of meat scraps. After setting the food on the ground, he needed to use the railing to pull himself back up, struggling to hold up his weight as the dogs scrapped over the contents of the plate. They were different breeds and ages and all had at least one visible injury: a missing ear on one, only three legs on another, and lesions all around. Through my lens, I could even see burn marks on them. What kind of person keeps that many dogs just to abuse them?

A few minutes later, he walked out of his house and down his front path. Wherever he was going, it appeared he was doing so on foot. His destination would need to be close with the shape he was in. I decided to follow him but gave him plenty of space. He walked into a check cashing store and handed over a check that appeared to be government-issued. He received his cash and bought booze and cigarettes, immediately lighting one up as he headed to the nearby grocery store. The man filled his shopping cart with frozen fried food, chips, soda, and cookies. I'm not sure if there was one thing in the cart that was even remotely healthy. Without hesitation, he made his way past the pet food aisle and spent twenty minutes in the bakery gathering enough sweets to feed a troupe of partying kids.

Standing by the checkout, he fingered through some awful magazine that was pushing stories of aliens and three-headed infants. He started to sweat as he loaded his groceries on the conveyor belt. When he was done, he had to waddle back out of the lane to wheel his cart past the cashier. He pulled out his wallet from the back pocket of stain-covered sweatpants. I made a game trying to identify each stain in the fabric.

Mustard. Coffee. Chocolate. Either ketchup or blood.

I followed him home, planning ways to end his sad excuse for a life.

Chapter 26

LYDIA

I head to Adam's, ready to tell him everything. So many things that I've never had the courage to say out loud and secrets that I've wanted to reveal but couldn't without the right sympathetic ear. My cheeks start to feel stiff, and I discover that I'm smiling. It isn't a forced smile, but a dumb, effortless smile that you don't realize you're wearing until it hurts your cheeks, and who knows how long you've had it plastered on your face. I might actually have a shot at being happy.

I turn the corner by the station when I hear my name being called somewhere behind me.

"Lydia! Lydia!"

I turn my head and spot Frank standing in front of the station doors waving his arms. Maybe an apology for what transpired in the interrogation. He should know at this point I don't need nor want it.

"What's going on?" I ask.

"A man has been discovered murdered in his home with multiple stab wounds."

He wouldn't be telling me this unless he thought it had something to do with our case. But home invasion doesn't fit our killer's pattern.

He continues. "Two uniformed officers arrived at the house to follow up on a noise complaint that had been filed days earlier. We're not sure how long the corpse has been there. The killer cranked the heating system all the way up to make the body decompose more rapidly. The officers ran out of the house before they really saw anything, but we know he was left sitting in a recliner chair."

"And you think it's our guy? He's only ever attacked victims in the woods."

"Yeah, but we also assumed he only hunted them here in Portland."

"Photos?"

"Apparently."

Having pondered what Adam's been up to the past week, I think I may have found my answer.

"My camera is at home," I say. "I'll run home, grab my gear, and meet you at the scene."

"I'll just drive you. It'll be quicker."

With that, he walks over to his car, opens the passenger door, then hustles to the other side.

It's a dreary ride to my apartment since the city is gridlocked. It almost doesn't matter what time of day you try. During the week, the streets are filled with moving trucks, delivery vans, bikers, pedestrians, and cars.

There's a panhandler set up on most street corners with a sign asking for help, his tent set up under the nearest overpass or in a vacant lot. It would probably have been quicker for me to walk.

When we arrive, I get out of the car in a flash and run up to my apartment door. I insert my key and hear Frank's door slam.

I look at him, waiting for an explanation, considering he's never come up to my place before.

"I left the station so fast I didn't have time to take a leak. Can I use your bathroom?" He can't seem to stand still. It's mildly amusing.

I have to think of a lie and fast. I've got photos on display of not only the victims in this case but also of all the cases since I started this job, and there's no time to strip every wall in my apartment.

"Actually... no," I say. "The plumbing is all out of whack. The landlord is supposed to get a plumber in here today or tomorrow. That laundromat has a bathroom." I gesture to the door next to mine. "I'm sure it won't be for long. I'll be right back."

I shut the door behind me and sigh with relief. I don't want to wait for the elevator and need to let out some steam, so I run up the four flights of stairs to my apartment. I close my door behind me and take off the necklace from Adam, hanging it on the coat rack. I take down all of my photos for the third time in as many weeks and stash them under the area rug. I change the memory card out of my camera and I'm out the door and running down the stairs out onto the street. Frank's waiting in the car and ready to go.

The house is only about ten blocks from mine, but it still takes us twenty minutes to get there. It's located on a side street near Woodstock. The house sticks out like a sore thumb on this street, lined with attractive houses. We pull up and notice a few officers standing out front, sweating even though it's cool outside. They cover their mouths with their jackets to protect against the smell.

We make our way up the sidewalk after putting on some hazardous materials gear. I notice a brick-colored streak of old blood leading to a nearby trash can on the sidewalk and snap my first shot at the scene. A detective from the station, Robert Clyde, whom Frank and I have known for years, is pale, and I can see the beads of sweat running down his face from ten feet away. He keeps having to remove his glasses to wipe away the condensation and keep them from sliding off his nose.

"You might want to wait a few minutes to let it air out more. The only thing we've done is open the few windows we could get to," Detective Clyde mutters between coughs.

"I can handle it if you can, Frank," I challenge.

"I can handle it," he tells me, then turns to Robert. "What do we know about the victim?"

"The victim's name is Lewis Allen. A noise complaint was filed a few days ago and those two came over today for a routine visit. Poor guys. They had no idea what they were in for." His gaze moves across the lawn to a pair of officers leaning over with their hands on their knees, vomit stains evident on their pants and shoes.

"Is it really that bad there?" Frank says. "I'm surprised by how weak their stomachs are."

"It's bad if you're not wearing that hazmat suit. You two should be fine."

Frank asks if I'm ready, though I assume he's asking himself more than me. We walk up the unstable wooden steps of the porch and stop inches from the front door to exchange glances.

I enter first.

Stacks of all sorts of paper reach head height. Magazines, newspapers, and broken-down cardboard boxes are layered precariously, one stack supporting the next and collapsing back onto walls they used to lean against. The stacks block my line of sight into the living room and make it impossible to enter through that doorway, so I move toward the kitchen. I take photos as I move along, trying not to step in the piles of spilled food or the animal feces that are scattered on the floor.

There's no ventilation in the kitchen, I guess the officers haven't made it this far back. With the heat up to ninety degrees, it's stifling in here. The smell is aggressive, lingering at the edges of my mask, so foul and cloying that I can taste hints of it with each inhalation. The countertops are stacked with crusty plates and filthy glasses gray with water stains. Scraps of food on the plates are unrecognizable, covered as they are in mold.

I try not to let my limbs graze any surface in there; I'd end up walking away with a collection of roving ants or cockroaches. I take some more photographs and gasp as I walk by the hall bathroom. Feces-streaked toilet paper overflowed out of the toilet and onto the floor. It's stacked high on top of the tank and covers the floor behind the unit. Some pieces are so old they've hardened in layers onto the bowl.

I try to steady my camera and capture the room so I can move on. The stairs are long since caved in, so I skip them as they're too dangerous to try presently. Besides, the man I'm looking for was found in the living room. There's no need for me to explore the cavernous filth of the house any more than necessary. We come around the corner and I lay eyes on him. I have to steady myself against the doorframe at the disgusting sight before me.

Bile rises out of my throat, and I fight it back down. The large man is sunk deep into his recliner, and from my angle, the glow of the television provides a bluish highlight on his face. It's difficult to make out the pool of blood until the shades are drawn and the stark afternoon light can shine onto him. The remote has been placed in his right hand and the left is stuffed in a bag of potato chips. The face is propped with chin down so his eyes are fixed on the television.

His t-shirt, full of holes, is drenched in blood. Multiple stab wounds line his chest, abdomen, arms, hands, and even some in his face. With the other victims, the wounds were limited to clean punctures, the blade was typically applied and removed at similar angles, perpendicular to the flesh. With this victim, the blade was dragged across his stomach, tearing through layers of skin and muscle tissue, if not the organs. This makes the largest wound to date—over a foot long.

On the floor lie over thirty photographs. So many—more at this crime scene than at all the other scenes combined—and some marked with the word "LIES".

"It's him," Frank says. "He's officially moved into the city."

One of the photos shows the man at home with a bunch of mangy dogs in the backyard. Several images reveal the dogs' injuries—tufts of fur missing, burn marks, missing limbs, missing eyes.

Somehow, they trusted Adam enough to get that close.

"Frank, have you seen or heard any signs of dogs since we got here?" I ask.

"Apparently, the neighbors complained often about dogs barking late into the night. But when the officers showed up today and found him, they couldn't find any dogs."

"He must have set them free."

"What a hero," he says sarcastically.

"I'll check the backyard, then come back in to finish up."

I make my way out the backdoor and my foot crashes through a rotten board, almost taking me down. At his size, I'm surprised any part of the porch is still standing.

Taking off my mask, I get a whiff of dog food as I walk around to the backyard.

The back gate stands open, and it looks as if it rained empty bags of dog food. Stiff, crumpled bags lay torn to pieces, littering the lawn. Our killer—Adam—fed, then freed the dogs. Based on Adam's pattern for killing and the photographs laying at the dead man's feet, I deduced that the victim was starving and torturing his animals.

I walk back inside, joining Frank by his side to resume documenting the case.

"If you want an accurate time of death," I say, "you might want to check with animal control. If we find out when a bunch of dogs got loose in the neighborhood, it might help give us a more accurate timeline."

"I'll call animal control to see if any dogs were picked up over the last week."

He's actually listening to me, beginning to see me as an equal.

Frank kneels to inspect the photographs.

"These dogs look terrible. Mistreated. Starved." He goes silent, then stands. "You a dog lover?"

"I can barely take care of myself, Frank."

"Well, I am."

He'll never say it, but I know what he's thinking.

Adam did the world a service.

I photograph every angle of the body before the medical examiner's team comes in to remove it. This proves exceedingly difficult since the man is over five hundred pounds and the stretcher can't fit through the front door. They have to demo the front bay window in order to get him out. As half a dozen men attempt to lift the body off of the recliner and onto the stretcher, bodily fluid from the man sluices out onto the floor. Since the speed of decomposition was artificially increased with heat, it shouldn't be that shocking to a room full of people used to seeing bodies, but in that moment every one of us gags.

I stand in front of the site formerly occupied by the bay window and take a gulp of the fall air. I love this time of year. I can smell smoke from some distant chimney. I watch as the leaves fall from their trees, their rich earthy tones staining the pavement with the colorful debris of a season past its prime. I decide to exit the house the same way the corpse did so I don't have to linger near the revolting stench of his life anymore.

When I get home, it takes me hours of scrubbing to rid myself of the stink of the cadaver and his hoarder house. I took a shower at the station but needed to take another once I arrived home.

I step onto the bath rug and wrap myself in a towel. I wipe my hand across the mirror so I can see a faint impression of my face behind the steam.

I take Adam's necklace off the coat rack and fasten it around my neck, preparing myself to call him.

He picks up on the second ring.

"Hello?"

An odd greeting, considering he should know it's me.

"Hi, Adam."

"It's been a while," he replies curtly. "I was beginning to think you'd lost interest in me."

"Can you come over?"

A moment of silence follows, and for a moment I think he's hung up.

"When?" he asks.

"Now."

"Okay… I need to take care of a few things, but I can come over in a few hours."

"Just buzz my door when you get here."

"Okay."

He hangs up, and I can picture his confusion. He won't know what he's walking into. After he finds out everything, I wonder if he'll still want me.

Since the morning I found the photograph of myself hidden in his bookshelf, I've been accosted by conflicting feelings about Adam and about my harmful past. If Adam is as similar to me as I think he is, he's likely never completely opened up to another person. Never revealed his dark side.

I dry my hair and sit out on my fire escape, looking at the trees in the distance and the skyline beyond. I know that once Adam comes over tonight, our lives will never be the same. I sit back against the cool bricks and wait, for the first time looking forward to what the future might bring.

The buzzer sounds.

Crawling in from the fire escape, I almost bang my head against the window. I press the buzzer and stand there, staring at the door. I wonder if he will take the stairs or the elevator. I creep close to the door and put my ear to it and close my eyes. In the distance, I can faintly hear footsteps shuffling up the stairs and as he gets closer, my eyes shoot open as feelings of nervousness and excitement run through my body. I step back from the door, and he knocks twice.

I open the door and it feels like we've been apart for months rather than a week. He looks different, darker, and not as vulnerable as he was the morning I left him. He's wearing a pair of blue jeans with black shoes and a white tee shirt with a black-and-gray striped zip-up hoodie over it all. He has a shorter and cleaner haircut but evidently hasn't shaved in a few days. His eyes are cold, and he definitely has no idea that I've just spent half of the day photographing the mess he left behind.

"Thanks for coming by."

"What's this about, Lydia? It's been over a week and call out of the blue asking me to rush over to your place?" He sounds irritated already as he walks over to the window with his back to me.

"You remember the case I've been working on?" It might be a little entertaining to make him squirm. I'm the only person who has dirt on him, maybe the only one to ever have had some type of control over him. "It's been a whirlwind over the last week."

"I wished you would have called me back. I know how important your job is to—"

"Another victim was discovered today."

Adam hesitates. "I'm sorry."

"I'm not so sure I am," I say.

He tilts his head, unsure how to respond.

"Seems like he was a pretty bad guy. A waste of a human being. An animal abuser by all accounts, if the photographs are any indication."

He looks away from me. "You're not supposed to tell me details about the case."

"I don't think there's anything I can tell you that you don't already know. Isn't that right, Adam?"

He hides his face, trying to avoid me from seeing he's gone pale, but I do.

I move to the left side of the couch and pull out two folders from under it.

"What are those?" he asks, pointing down at the folders, not knowing that they're filled with photographs of all of the people he's killed, including Heather and Jacob. "I wanted you to get an inside look into the case I've been working on for the past few weeks. I know I said I couldn't show you before, but part of me... *really* feels like you'll understand what I've been going through if you see them."

I wonder if he'll react. I'm playing a dangerous game right now, baiting him, but I need to give him one breadcrumb at a time.

I take one of the folders over to the rug and sit down, gesturing for him to do the same. He hesitates at first, and then agrees to sit down across from me. I set apart my favorite photographs from each of the crime scenes, up until Heather and Jacob.

He looks at them with a forced expression of remorse and sympathy, as if he's hiding his true feelings.

I point to the mannequin-like bodies of Heather and Jacob and look at him. "That was my foster sister Heather and my nephew Jacob." I don't look away from his eyes. He wants to say something but doesn't know what. He's waiting for more from me.

"You already know that. Don't you, Adam?" I try to keep my voice as steady as I can.

"Lydia... I'm so sorry, but I don't know what you're talking about. I think you've been watching too many crime shows."

"Don't play dumb, Adam. No more lying. You shouldn't be exempt from your own rules. Don't be what you're trying to rid the world of."

It's only natural that he'd try to protect himself. Still, I'm disgusted at this lack of honesty.

He rises to his feet and walks towards the front door. Before he can open it, I move in front of him.

"Tell me the truth, Adam. I think you owe me that much."

He steps back, sauntering deeper into my apartment until he falls to the couch. "I had no idea they were your sister and nephew. I didn't see you two together the day I met you."

"So when did you find out? Was it after you killed them or before?"

"You don't want to hear this. You really don't."

"Adam, please. I need to know."

He looks past my shoulder to the front door again. "You know what I've done... and yet you're here with me alone in an enclosed space."

"You won't hurt me. I know you won't. Have you heard a single police siren? You think I'd have you come over here just to see you walk out in handcuffs?"

"Then what do you want from me?"

"I want you to be honest with me. Don't leave a single detail out. Tell me how they died."

Adam casts his eyes down. He starts to tell me everything.

"You already know that I drug my victims. It was the same with them; I started with Jacob since he was sleeping near the river at the time. After I drugged him, I carried him over to the campsite."

Tears well up in my eyes as he describes Jacob's last moments.

"Are you sure you want me to go on?"

I nod.

"Your foster sister abandoned him in the woods so she could snort lines off the hood of her car. She was a drug addict who physically and emotionally abused her son in the few hours I was observing them. Once someone figured her out, Jacob would have gone into the system. I've been through that, I didn't want that for him.

"I didn't find the photograph until after I killed them. I swear I didn't. I went back to the car to take a picture, and my flashlight caught it. I just froze in place. I stood there holding the photograph of you, wondering what the hell I should do next. I wanted so badly to tell you that night you came over to my place... Can you forgive me?"

After hearing his explanation, I know it's time to tell him my secret. If I can manage through the tears. I begin to cry uncontrollably, and my body starts to shake.

Adam sits on the floor next to me and puts me in his lap, holding me tight. After a few minutes, I can finally breathe normally again. I pull my face away from the nook formed by his arm and shoulder and stare at him.

"I'm so sorry that I hurt you... but I'm not sorry for what I did," he says. "That's the truth. Can you live with that? With me being this person?"

"I'm not afraid of living with the person you are. I'm more afraid you won't be able to accept me for mine."

He looks at me without understanding.

"You're not the only person that's guilty of murder," I say.

Chapter 27

ADAM

I look at her tear-stained face, full of fear and guilt. I'm not sure that I heard her right, and I have no idea what she'll say next, but I need to know what it is that torments her. We're much more alike than I had thought.

"What did you just say?" I ask.

"I've killed before. It's probably my most vivid memory from those years, smelling the smoke rising off the house, the flames licking at the cloud cover in the early morning. I sat in front of their house, hoping it would all burn so quickly that the only thing left would be their charcoal remains."

"Who?" Then it hits me. "You blame yourself for what happened to your foster parents?"

"I wanted to kill *her* too. Heather was supposed to be in the house, but

I found her outside on the lawn."

"Are you saying, you... started the fire?"

She looks at me, fearing my judgment.

"Lydia," I say, "I'm here and I'm listening. Why would you want to kill them?" I place my hands over hers.

"I want to tell you everything, but I'm scared you won't understand."

"I think we've both been scared of that our entire lives. I won't judge and I won't leave. I'll listen to every word you have to say."

"I can't tell you about all the shitty foster homes I've been in because I can't remember them all, but I'll tell you about the last one.

"I lived with Heather and her family for almost two years. I was twelve when I went to live with them. I remember it was during the fall, my favorite season, because not long after I arrived, Heather and I were riding our bikes around the neighborhood on Halloween. We thought it'd be fun for me to go as Elliot and her to go as E.T. Her father was usually drunk at a bar until ten or eleven and we knew that her mom would let us go trick-or-treating as long as we threw out the costumes and hid our candy."

She tells the story with a sad smile and it's easy to understand that this was the high point for her. Knowing this will soon go downhill, I brace myself.

"That was the only time I remember being happy until I drove away from Seattle, the day I turned eighteen. I went into a group home after the fire and threatened my social worker with defiance and unruly behavior if she ever tried to place me again."

"Jesus. What the fuck did he do to you? That you not only wanted to kill him but the entire family."

She visibly recoils from me. It's incredible how much she's survived.

She brings her legs into her chest and wraps her arms tightly around them. She stares out the window, but not at anything in particular.

"Lydia. Tell me what happened. I want to know. I want to be here for you if you want me to be. I think you're incredible for your resolve. I just want to understand."

I wait to see what bits and pieces she'll share next.

"Heather is a few years younger than me, and it took me several months to figure out the real reason I was brought into their home. I was there for him. Her mother had noticed the way he was looking at Heather at the dinner table and the way he'd stare into her bedroom at night. He'd stand in the doorway with a beer bottle in one hand and the other hand down his pants watching her while he touched himself."

She pauses and holds her stomach with both hands with a queasy look on her face.

"I'll never forget the day I arrived. She told me that Heather would be staying downstairs on the couch and I'd get my very own room. I'd never had my own room, so of course I felt honored and excited. I ran my fingers along every surface in that room and I loved to close the door and dance around in circles. I finally had somewhere quiet to read and concentrate. It was a dream come true for someone raised in close quarters with child strangers. In those few months, I actually started to feel happy for the first time in my life... Until the first visit from him."

She lifts herself onto the couch deliberately and curls up on one of the arms like it's taking every ounce of her energy to tell this story.

"I actually preferred it when he raped me from behind. At least then I didn't have to smell his breath or watch him as he did it. I could bury my face in the pillow and escape into my head. The next morning, I went downstairs feeling sore and scared. Heather was already off playing outside, but her mother was sitting at the table with a grim expression on her face. She had made me breakfast.

"'I made you pancakes, eggs, French toast, and bacon. I didn't know what your favorite breakfast food was, but I can make you whatever you'd like,' she told me.

"I sat down with a piece of dry toast and nibbled off a corner of it, not looking at her and not saying a word. She had the nerve to tell me then that I was saving the family. That she had made a choice to do this in order to save her own daughter. I wasn't a foster child to her. I was armor for her little girl to wear against a lecherous monster.

"Things stayed that way for almost two years. He was consistent, visiting at least once a week, and I'd had enough. I became kind of obsessed with true crime at an early age. When TV shows about people using forensic science to solve violent crimes started airing in the early 90s, I was hooked. Heather's mother watched it all the time."

She seems eager now—almost excited—to share the rest about how she conquered her fear and made her way out of the darkness and through the flames.

"I know the show you're talking about. A little cheesy but the cases are interesting because they're true. So you took notes?"

"So I took notes." She smiles and looks at me. It's the first time she has in a while.

"How did you get away with it?"

"Well... Heather's mother took Valium at night to help with her anxiety and depression, so I knew she'd sleep right through. He was a chain smoker and a drunk, so I just had to wait for a night where he wasn't too drunk to make it up the stairs. Some nights he'd pass out on the kitchen floor, and others he wouldn't even make it in the house."

I thought back to living with my uncle, him being too drunk to function and surrounding him with his own switchblades. I couldn't wait to tell her.

"The lucky night arrived, and he headed up the stairs. I'd hoped he wouldn't come into my room that night, but he did. I suffered through it more easily than I had in the past since I knew it'd be the last time. I thought of him burning to death as he thrust himself into me. He left my room and went to bed. I saw the glow of the TV from the hall outside their room and knew he was going to drink more beer and smoke cigarettes in bed until he passed out. The son of a bitch actually kept a cooler in the bedroom. I waited another hour and crawled out along the floor into their bedroom. He was snoring loudly, and I could see the ember of his cigarette. I moved his ashtray so that the ash from the cigarette would drop directly onto the carpet. He kept lighter fluid on the nightstand for an old Zippo he'd had since high school. I opened the can of fluid and tipped it so it would soak the floor. I pushed the filter of the cigarette out of his hand with a bobby pin from her nightstand. I knew that at that point I didn't have a lot of time. I made for the door."

"What if they woke up and tried to escape the house?"

"She wouldn't—I knew that much—since she almost always took double her dose, probably to block out his horrible advances. He may have tried to stumble to safety, but I had figured that he would fall down the stairs if he even made it that far and that was my worst-case scenario. Sometimes the door to their bedroom was difficult to open, and the lock would stick. I loosened a screw so they wouldn't be locked in exactly, but it would make it more difficult for them to get out. I knew it would be strange if they found Heather locked in my room. Most nights, her mother gave her medication to help her stay asleep on the couch and to prevent her from sleepwalking. I made sure that she got an extra pill that night. He liked to try and cook nights when he was wasted, so I turned one of the burners on but not all the way so the kitchen would fill with gas. I walked out the front door, sat on the lawn, and waited."

"So, Heather was the only one to make it out?"

"Yeah... I found her sleeping on the back lawn. She must have woken up somehow, either from the smell of the gas or maybe from all of the noise of the fire upstairs. I should have killed her then, but I wasn't able to. She didn't do anything to hurt me directly, but it was her virginity and her existence that I was protecting, that led to my living hell. That's why I had wanted her to die in the fire too. She was the only family I had left, but she was also a constant reminder of him and those two years."

"And you've never told anyone before?"

"Of course not. I killed two people. No one would understand. No one besides... you... After I found out that you're the killer we've been looking for, I had all of these conflicting emotions. I'm sure you can imagine. But in spite of what you are and what you've done, I can't let you go. There is something between us that I can't deny and won't walk away from. There were times at the crime scenes when I tried to get into your head. The detectives and agents didn't understand how I was making these accurate assumptions. They didn't have the capacity to understand you and why you're killing."

"So what is your conclusion, Miss Walker? Why do I do it?"

"I think you owe me an explanation now, don't you? After all, I did just bare my soul to you after accusing you of multiple homicides, and somehow we're both still here."

"That's fair. What do you want to know?"

Chapter 28

LYDIA

I can't believe he's still sitting in front of me. Though he's killed too, I didn't assume he'd be accepting of my dark confessions. I'm not sure what I thought would happen from this point. The more we open up to each other now, the more it seems like we're strengthening this twisted relationship.

"I don't really know where to start, to be honest," I say. "Is this the first time in your life you've ever killed anyone?"

I've been so obsessed with true crime and the minds of serial killers, but I've never had a chance to interview one, if that's what I'm doing with Adam now. And on top of that, he's a guy that I'm completely hooked on.

"Yes. The couple was the first. I was fed up with people lying to me. I started to understand at an early age that people often have no remorse for their lies. Eventually, I realized I could retaliate with violence."

"How were you lied to as a child?"

"My whole home life was a lie. The woman that I thought of as my sister turned out to be my biological mother. And the two people whose house I grew up in, who I treated like my parents, were actually my aunt and uncle. He was a drunk and used to beat my aunt."

He smiles then, and it's a devious smile. A memory he's reliving that makes him pleased with himself.

"What are you thinking about right now?"

"I had a sick sense of humor, especially against the people who lied to me. After he hit my aunt one day and passed out on the living room floor, I decided I'd have a little fun with his switchblade collection. He used to travel to knife shows around the state looking for different switchblades."

"You use a different switchblade at each crime scene?"

"Yeah... Thinking of him now, I know I would have ended up killing him if he hadn't killed himself first."

"He committed suicide?"

"Well, not exactly. He was coming home from the local bar during a blizzard and slipped on some ice only a few feet from our front door. Son of a bitch froze to death," he laughs.

"It sounds like he had it coming to him. What happened on the living room floor when he passed out?"

"After he passed out, I took all of his switchblades and placed them carefully around his body, head to toe. Each of the pointy blades was less than an inch from some part of him. One was right in front of his eyes. I sat up on the couch and waited for him to wake up. It was exciting to think that I could cause him so much pain and the best part was he deserved it."

"So why start killing now?"

The conversation unfolds so naturally it doesn't feel as if we're talking about his violent behavior, but rather something as nonchalant as what his favorite books were when he was little.

"I've only had strong feelings for a woman once before meeting you. It was a fraction of what I feel for you, but at the time it was more than I'd ever felt for anyone. I had never let anyone get close to me before that."

"I've never felt as if I could be myself with any of the guys I've tried to date. It was always casual, and I never had them over to my place. If I ever even alluded to anything un-feminine or remotely dark, they'd say my interest was a turnoff or that they didn't understand why I was into 'all that stuff.' I started to shut down. I couldn't win, so I stopped trying. I almost walked away from you."

"That's exactly how it felt with Lauren. She never understood me, never showed any interest in my book dealing or collecting. I got a bit carried away in the bedroom with her and she grabbed her clothes and left. I only saw her once after that."

"What did you do to her?" I'm scared to ask, but I have to know.

"We were being rough during sex, and she said I could choke her, but it's a dangerous game. There was something so arousing to know I could choke the life out of her, and it turned me on so much that I didn't hear her gasping for air. I didn't feel her hitting me until it was almost too late. She crawled off the bed and looked at me. Devastated or disgusted, I'm not sure. That wasn't the worst part, though."

He runs his fingers through his hair and grabs the back of his neck with both hands, placing his elbows on his knees.

"We met for coffee a few weeks later and she said I was sick and that there was something seriously wrong with me. That I was 'fucked up in the head' and no one would ever accept me for me, so I should look forward to dying alone."

"Wow, that's pretty rough. I mean, I could understand being scared in that situation, but she didn't even try to understand?"

"Would you if I almost killed you?"

"I don't know. I haven't been afraid of dying in a long time. I'm not suicidal or anything just... indifferent."

"You've survived so much, though."

"I still have to live with everything I survived, and sometimes it feels like it's almost too much to bear."

"Well, I guess I'll have to care about your life if you don't. When Lauren said all of those things, I thought that she was right. My mother rejected me in the same way before she sent me to live in the foster home. She accused me of being soulless and called me a monster. When I heard it from Lauren too, I just snapped. I was sick of trying to be this version of myself that I hoped others would like. I wanted to be me, and I started to think about when I felt the most like myself and it was when I was a kid sitting on the couch, staring at my uncle and waiting for him to get what was coming to him."

"You seem like you'd always been upset at your mother and family for lying to you though. It still doesn't make sense to me. Why now."

He chuckles. "I'm getting there... After I met with Lauren that day, the conversation wouldn't leave my head. A few weeks later, I found myself in an outdoor goods store listening to this couple fighting... Then they dropped it and acted like everything was fine. He was a pushover, resorted to ignoring her ugliness instead of standing up to it, and she was whiny and vain, berating him needlessly. They were fake. At that moment I believed that, since they were lying to themselves and not living truthfully, there was no point to them living at all."

"That's... one way to rationalize serial murder," I say. "I'm going to play devil's advocate if that's fine by you."

"Try me," he says.

"I can understand that you'd be frustrated with their conversation... but why decide to kill them? A lot of people infuriate me on a daily basis, but I don't go around killing them."

"Maybe you should."

"I'm trying to ask you a serious question."

"I'm being serious. Look, each and every person I've killed has deserved it."

"And the children?"

"Won't have to live with the lies and suffering any longer."

"You don't know that for sure."

"You're right. I don't. I don't think for a second that I do it only to punish others. I do it because it makes me feel alive. Having that much power, it's... incredible. I do it to let out all the hatred I still have toward my family for lying to me. But I also do it because I never want anyone to go through what I did. To have to carry that around with them... You sat there and told me the story of how you'd killed your foster parents. You didn't seem upset. There was pride in your voice. Didn't it feel *good*? Didn't it bring you a sense of relief?"

"Of course it did, but he physically, emotionally, and sexually abused me. These people haven't done anything to you, and that's the difference."

"You killed your foster mother and wanted to kill your foster sister too, though. They didn't directly hurt you. They were just reminders of the horrible life you lived."

Was he right? Did I enjoy it too much? I've attempted to bury horrible flashbacks of being raped by reminding myself of how incredibly freeing it felt to end my foster father's life.

"If Heather's mother had had the courage to leave him when she thought he may start molesting their daughter," I say, "I would've never lived with them in the first place. Heather I hated because she always thought she had the best dad ever. She named her goddamn child after him."

"Maybe you'd let go of some of that tension if you joined me. I know it helped me."

"I just don't think I could kill someone who hasn't directly hurt me."

A long silence lingers in my apartment.

"So, what do we do now?" he asks.

Chapter 29

LYDIA

It's been a few weeks since Adam and I bared our souls to one another. I've begun holding college classes again, with newfound confidence. I've had an inside look into the mind of a serial killer, and after class, I've been going home to him.

I'm not sure if I can join him like he hopes I will, or how I'll feel about everything if I stay out of it. He hasn't pressured me. The last week has been filled with lazy days where we read and lounge and drink coffee. We take walks in the nearby neighborhoods, we watch films, and we make love. He sprinkles hints into our conversations, into our pillow talk. Implications that should make my skin crawl but don't.

I lay in his bed in the same sweater I wore on our first date, having fallen asleep in it with college papers in my lap and a red pen in my hand. The sun beams through his balcony door like it always does, and it warms my face enough to drive me out of bed.

I walk down the hall to lean inside the doorway of Adam's study. Adam has five rare books on his desk, all open to random pages, and he's taking photographs of them in different lights. He smiles and walks over to me. He brushes my hair off my shoulder so he can hold my cheek in his hand.

"What do you want to do tonight?"

"I have some papers to grade, but I can do that later. The sun is still out and it's a beautiful evening. Let's go for a walk and maybe take some photos."

"I'll get our cameras ready and meet you downstairs."

"Give me five minutes."

We stop to grab slices of pizza to eat while we walk around the neighborhood, looking like tourists, each with a camera hung from our necks. The trees are filled with leaves in different shades of yellow, red, and orange. I love the outliers that are in the mix: a few greens too stubborn to change and conversely some browns that were too eager.

I glance over at Adam. I can't read him, which is unsettling. He has been quiet since that night. We've had so much fun over the past few weeks, but I feel him growing distant from me. He's holding back, and he thinks he's doing it for me. But I know what he needs.

We walk down one of the busier streets lined with restaurants and bars, between residential neighborhoods.

I halt to a stop and Adam follows my gaze.

Across the street outside of a restaurant, a middle-aged man is yelling at a woman. His speech is slurred and he's swaying from side to side. He's wearing a suit, and the woman is in a dress with an open sweater and a scarf wrapped around her neck, an unnecessary concession against her outfit considering it's only fifty degrees outside. He's twice her size and wide enough that she would disappear behind his bulk if they stood just right.

He has her by the arm and is shaking her so hard that she drops her purse. With wrath, he lets go of her and she slams against the brick wall. Bracing for more, she falters, then starts to pick up the spilled contents of her purse. The sweater she's wearing falls off of one shoulder, exposing a blue bruise that stretches over her arm and appears to travel both downward beneath the dress and upward under the scarf.

"I can't believe he has the nerve to treat her like that at all, let alone in public," Adam says. "Look at all the people passing by. They must hear what he's saying to her. Hell, they're only a few feet from them."

"That's the way *he* used to treat all of us when he drank... When he would force himself on me."

I can't take my eyes off of them. The woman catches me staring and hurries, collecting the contents of her purse and rising unsteadily. She tries to coax him into walking away from the busy street.

I pull Adam's arm and glance back at him and then at the couple. I want to follow them. He smiles as if he can read my mind, but he doesn't know what I'm thinking. Not exactly. I don't want to kill him. I just want to follow him.

When I don't return his smile, his cheeks sag.

"We're only going to watch from a distance," I say.

"Yeah, we'll just take a walk."

"Is that what you did with the last victim?"

"What, follow him?"

"Yes."

"I was actually out for a walk just like this and heard a dog whimper and yelp. I circled the block, and when I came back down the street, he was dragging a trash bag with what looked to be blood streaking the sidewalk. I knew what he'd done. I wanted to kill him right there, but I needed a plan."

"So then you came back the next day?"

"Yeah, and the more I found out about him, the more sure I was that he deserved it. No one misses that sad excuse for a man. And no more animals have had to die."

"I have to admit, that was the first of your crime scenes where no one seemed sympathetic to the victim."

"I take the most pride in regards to that murder above all the others. It wasn't my first, and so I had a good idea of what it would take to accomplish my goal. I was able to familiarize myself with him and found nothing redeeming. I had fleeting doubts when I was stalking the other victims, but he just kept adding to the laundry list of shittiness that made up his life. It was liberating to kill him."

We walk two or three streets into a quiet neighborhood. The man opens a gate to a walkway leading up to a house. The woman is fumbling around in her purse, I think for her keys, when he takes hold of her hair and drags her body to the door. I walk a few steps in front of Adam and let go of his hand, but he grasps it tighter and tugs me back into place with him at the street corner. I frown, wanting an explanation of why we can't move closer.

"We have to wait until they get inside. We can't follow too closely. They'll notice us."

"That drunk piece of shit isn't going to notice a damn thing."

I'm surprised by how angry I feel. I'm sure I've passed couples arguing before. Maybe my newfound anger is showing itself now because of things with Adam and the finality I feel from Heather and Jacob's deaths. Emotions that have been dormant for years are coming to the surface. I feel powerful and capable enough to face this with him beside me.

"You don't think we look suspicious as it is, standing here on a corner and staring at a house?"

He laces his fingers around my waist and pulls me in, clacking our cameras together. "We might just be lovers of good architecture." He kisses me on my neck. "Or we're looking to buy our own wholesome house, and this is our way of finding inspiration." He kisses me on the other side of my neck, then places a sweet, comforting kiss on my lips.

He peers over toward the house. "They're inside."

I raise my camera. "Then let's have a closer look."

Chapter 30

ADAM

We walk around the block to see if we can gain a better vantage point, somewhere other than right behind a tree. I let go of Lydia's hand and she doesn't hesitate to climb the tree.

She finds a sturdy spot and steadies her camera in her hands, staring through the viewfinder and gently twisting the zoom lens. She whispers down to me, "It's the perfect spot. We can see into the back of the house, some of the living room, a good angle on their kitchen, and the bedroom."

Perched on the branches, her upper body pivots as she scans each room.

"They're in the bedroom," she says grimly. "The woman's sitting on the bed and... she's sobbing."

"Where's the man?" I ask.

She pivots again. "He's in the kitchen, sipping from a glass... Liquor, it looks like... He's putting the glass down and heading upstairs." She draws a sharp breath.

"You don't have to watch this," I say.

"He's in the room now, saying—No, *yelling* something. She's... she's taking off her clothes, and... and lying on her stomach with her legs hanging off the bed." She turns her gaze away from the viewfinder.

"Lydia..." I say.

"No," she shoots back, bringing her eye to the viewfinder again. "He's tripping over himself." She groans, disgusted. "He just fell on top of the woman... He's undoing his pants..."

She looks away, for good this time, I think.

"You've seen enough," I say, holding my hand up towards her.

She climbs down rather recklessly, her body limp. When I catch her at the bottom, she says, "The woman... she was crying."

We walk quickly, making our way back to my house, saying nothing.

I shut the door and Lydia sits down on the couch in front of the fire. She doesn't look at me or say anything for a while. I sit on the floor near the fireplace and wait patiently for her to process everything she's just seen and all the memories it must bring back about her own abuse.

"I get it now. Everything you said earlier. I didn't think I could do it, but now after seeing him rape his own wife and degrade her like that... I can't go on living my life knowing that he's out there. That I could do something to end the suffering of that woman."

"So what do you want to do, Lydia?"

"I'm going to kill him, and you're going to help me," she declares.

Did she really understand what she was saying? If she feels the same tomorrow, I know we're going to have a lot of fun together. Maybe she can find an avenue through which to channel her pain.

Chapter 31

LYDIA

I woke up before Adam for the first time since I started sleeping here. From the balcony, I breathe in the crisp fall air and think about the day ahead.

Her life could be forever altered tonight.

I head inside and slip out of the room, so as not to wake Adam. After making a pot of coffee, I lounge around in his study, landing in the reading nook he set up for me with a stack of my books from home. I attempt to dive into the words of authors whose work has brought me comfort for so long, but the image of the crying woman, with her arms flat against the bed, overpowers the words on the page.

An hour or so later, Adam's feet press against the floorboards, then the stairs. A few minutes after that, he comes to find me in the study, his hair disheveled and wearing a t-shirt and boxer briefs. He holds two steaming cups of coffee and hands me one.

He's groggy but alert enough for what I'm about to ask him. "So, what do we need to do first?"

He takes a sip of coffee, breathing in while he sips, and breathes out afterward with a satisfied, "Ahhh."

"Before we make any sort of plan for tonight," he says. "I want to make sure you know what you're getting into. There's no backing out once we start. I never wore any kind of mask or disguise during the other crimes. I would do this so I wouldn't have any choice but to follow through. It never came up for me, but if I were in disguise, I would have had it in the back of my head that I could let them live."

I frown. "You don't think I'll go through with it, do you?"

"That's not it. You say you've killed before, but it wasn't intimate, it was indirect. You set a fire and they died as a result. This time, you are going to be looking into their eyes while you end their lives."

"*Their* lives?"

"Yes. Both of them."

I shake my head. "I only want *him* dead, Adam. I can't kill her.""It's the only way we can take away all of the horrible trauma she's experienced at his hands. Maybe even prevent her from falling in with another man just like him. If we kill her, she'll be released from having to live with the terrible memories."

"Those assumptions."

He downs another sip of coffee, getting impatient with me. "Do you not want to continue?"

I avoid the thought and continue. "There's definitely more risk with this couple since we don't know their schedules or what they've got going on this weekend. It's Friday, though, so our best case scenario is that no one will be looking for them until Monday or Tuesday. There's a lot to do before the day gets away from us. I want you to head over there and just walk around the block a few times. If you're able to discreetly look into the house for any details that may be helpful, do it. Do they have any animals? How many people live there? Are there multiple cars or do they have an alarm system? Things like that."

Adam relaxes in front of me, unmistakably impressed. "And what are you going to do while I'm out?"

"I'll be preparing a second bag for tonight," I say. "I need you to make me a list."

He nods, then smirks. "So, tonight's the night?"

"Tonight's the night," I answer.

I *will* end the man's life tonight. I just don't yet know what I'll do about the woman.

Chapter 32

ADAM

I head out of the house with my camera around my neck, walking with a bounce in my step. I never expected this. Not in my wildest dreams. I thought Lydia was everything I wanted before, but this new version of her—the one who's willing to venture into the darkest corners with me—is something extraordinary.

When I know I'm about a block away, I start to look for appropriate trees, ones I can stand under or hide by. I crouch across the street from the backside of their house, take a few street shots and some photos of the sky and the trees. Anyone would think I'm some amateur photographer out to get some lazy shots of the Portland suburbs.

As I walk by their house, I notice the garage door is open and empty, so the man is most likely at work. I cross over to a group of rose bushes and take a few macro shots, again playing the part. I look through the viewfinder, pretending to make adjustments, and the next time I put it to my eye, I raise it a few inches higher than the roses. Now I'm perfectly poised to see into the kitchen of their home.

The woman sits at the kitchen table holding tissues to her eyes and the phone to her ear. She's wearing a tank top and gym shorts, but at first glance looked like she was wearing a long sleeve shirt and pants. As I zoom in I can see that almost every inch of her exposed skin has bruises that range in color, which means he beats her almost every day. The bruise on her shoulder is blue and purple while another one on her forearm and wrist has a pale green tinge. I spot another on her thigh in a sickly yellowish-brown color. I scan around the house through my lens the best I can, looking for any helpful information for tonight. There doesn't appear to be an alarm system, no outside security camera system, and no sign of a dog, but it's difficult to tell with only one angle to work with. I look back to the woman and think she won't be depressed much longer. Soon she will be free of all the abuse she's been experiencing. She won't even have to contend with the past coming back to haunt her.

I take a few more shots and head back to my house.

I search for the address online and find that the residents are Connie and Mark Douglas. I fantasize about taking a knife and driving it through Mark Douglas' chest. That is, if Lydia doesn't do it first.

I shower, doing one quick scrub in preparation for a more thorough scrubbing later.

Afterward, I go out to my garage. I have one of those garage organizers, but it's really just a fancy door behind which I can hide everything I need for a kill. I move it out of the way and everything we'll need for the night is organized neatly on wooden shelving. I have four black backpacks, three different kinds of rope, rags and small bottles for chloroform, dozens of pairs of shoes bought at different times from shoe stores across Oregon and Washington, and a growing collection of black clothing. T-shirts, hoodies, sweatpants, jeans, jackets, hats, leather gloves, and socks—all black. Dozens of memory cards, camera lenses, instant cameras and film, and latex gloves fill more shelves. I take inventory after every kill so I can collect the items I'll need for future murders in my downtime. I never go to the same store more than once when I'm buying this stuff, and I always pay with cash.

My favorite part of this area is the glass display case where I've kept my uncle's switchblade collection. After that day of watching and waiting for him to wake up surrounded by his own blades, I knew I had to have them. Eventually, he died, and they were mine. I've used a different one for each set of murders. I think I'll have Lydia choose the knife she wants to use tonight.

Footsteps *creak* from above. Lydia is back.

"Down here!" I yell through the open garage entryway.

She appears with plastic bags of items, her forearms tense from the weight, and sets them down on the concrete in front of me. "That's everything," she says, panting.

I smile and nod. "Nice work."

"How'd your sweep of the house go?"

"It went well. We can go over the photos in a bit. There's still a lot to do. I need to make sure we're prepared."

Curiously, she circles around the garage, eyeing the objects, the clothes, the camera, until she spots the glass case and stops.

"These are the knives you use?" she asks, touching the case with care.

"Yes." I aim my finger toward the glass, wiping a line over four specific knives. "These are the ones I used."

"And these were the knives you described in your story with your uncle." It pleases me that she remembers such an important part of my past.

"Yes... and now, Lydia, I want you to pick the one you're going to use for tonight."

Her face turns to stone, and she scowls at the knives. I can tell she's envisioning her first kill.

"That one," she doesn't take long to decide and there's a certainty in her voice that dissuades me from questioning her choice.

I slide the case open and take the blade from its cradle with my gloves on.

"Why do you use gloves when you're going to put it back in the case?" she asks.

"I'm cautious. I try to plan for every scenario. What if I dropped it? If I was careless or surprised and the knife got left behind, it'd have my fingerprints all over it. I have to be one step ahead. Think about that while we're preparing. There's still a lot to go over before tonight."

"Then let's make some coffee and go to your study. You can fill me in there. It doesn't matter how small the detail is, Adam. I need to know all of it for us to be successful tonight."

"We'll be fine. I'm not worried. I'm quite excited to see you take the last breath from this lowlife."

She stands up and raises her chin, smiling. I kiss her softly and take her by the hand, leading us back into the house. We take cups of coffee up to my study and go over every detail meticulously. I want this to go as smoothly as possible since I've only had one successful attack in someone's home.

While Lydia and I go over the entire plan I watch for any signs of hesitation.

"I want to go through all of the notes one more time before we burn them."

"That's fine. The most important thing I want you to remember tonight is to stay focused. You can't let your emotions get the better of you or you're going to make a mistake."

"Tonight, when I thrust the knife into him, I'll be channeling all the rage and hatred toward this man and every man like him. But not a moment before."

The closer we get to tonight the more I can tell she's ready. I think she's been ready for a long time. She had to rid herself of the dead weight.

"You are so incredibly brave. You know that, right?" I say.

Her demeanor softens, but she rolls her eyes and starts to turn away from me. I grab her arm and turn her so she's facing me again.

"I'm not good at compliments," she says.

"You need to hear this and understand that I mean it." She looks up at me and I can see that the scared little girl from so many years ago is still with her.

"You are brave, and you have survived more than anyone should ever have to experience. You made him pay and now you'll make this man pay."

"Yes, I will. I feel like I was never quite comfortable in my own skin because of how people reacted to me. Now with you, I can finally be myself... And I'm not afraid of it."

I pull her into my arms and kiss her.

Chapter 33

LYDIA

I feel exhausted from all of tonight's preparations. After selecting the perfect switchblade, we went over the plan. I studied every detail, read and re-read, over and over until I had it memorized. Later I tore each sheet from the legal pad and threw it into the fire. I love sitting in front of his fireplace. The crackling sound and the heat of the flames remind me of my act of liberation and the night when I found the strength within myself. I will find it again tonight.

After we burned our notes, Adam and I showered. We scrubbed each other raw to lessen the chance that any hair or skin cells could be recovered by forensics. While we were in the shower, we went over the different scenarios that the evening might present to us. I felt ready.

I picked out a pair of athletic pants, a long-sleeved shirt, a hat, and cheap sneakers. While I didn't have much choice for color, other than black, he had every style of sporty clothing that any store would carry.

I stand behind the same tree as I was on the night I saw that man raping his wife. I saw her tears streaming down her face, staining their blanket. That image will always be with me, burned into my memory. It was like looking at myself from the outside. I used to be that helpless creature until I finally did something about it. I can do something for her too. Maybe she's too weak to fight it on her own.

"We can set her free from the devastating life she's been forced to live," Adam says. "If we get to her first, that makes things easier. Less weight to carry. If they're not together and we see him first, we'll have to get to her fast after we drug him. We can't risk the husband waking up."

"Adam... This doesn't feel right."

He sighs. "You want to call it off?"

"No, just... You've told me before that one of the reasons you kill the victims is that they're weak. Or because their future is hopeless... But look at us... Look at what we've been through. We got through living hell, and we made it out the other side. Why not give her a chance to do the same?"

He hesitates, looking irritated. "You should have brought this up before."

"I know."

He lowers his head in disappointment. "Lydia, if she sees us... You know we can't let her live. Are you prepared for that?"

I nod passively, still unsure. "I want to do this."

"Okay."

He approaches the house from the far side of the street and gives me a single nod. This means that we're going in through the back door. The front porch offers multiple options for windows, so we thought that we'd decide when we arrived since it would really depend on where in the house they were. Since he's in the living room and she's upstairs, it's evident that we should go through the back door. It's around ten on a Friday night, so there's some background noise that's audible from a few streets away working in our favor. I jump down from the tree, and we leap the fence into their backyard. Adam crawls up to the backdoor while I move around the side of the house and look into the living room. I see the shadow of a man in the light from the television. I nod once at Adam.

He picks the lock easily and I hurry along behind him before closing the back door without a sound. With the action film blaring over the surround sound in the living room, I hope the wife won't realize what's happening. She wouldn't dare come downstairs to ask him to turn it down. Adam sets his bag down on the floor in the hall.

The man is lying on the couch, and I can see the back of his head against one armrest. He can't see us coming from the hallway. Adam pulls out the chloroform and a rag. We'd decided earlier that Adam should be the one to drug him since the man's size left me at a distinct disadvantage.

But I'd be the one to kill him.

In one quick motion, Adam has the rag over the man's nose and mouth. His arms flail, bashing the lamp on the end table. I reach out for it and manage to catch it inches above the floor. Adam smiles at me approvingly, still holding the rag over the man's mouth. The man's arms finally go limp to the sounds of loud explosions and fast-paced music. It's like we have our own murder soundtrack.

Adam looks toward the stairs, contemplating whether to go after the wife. "She could come down the stairs any minute," he says, pulling the rope out of his bag.

The husband is unconscious, his entire weight folding into the couch. It would be easy to do it just like this, to have Adam cover his mouth while I force the blade into his skin. She wouldn't know a thing until she found him.

My heart races with anticipation.

I reach into my bag and find the handle of the knife. I grip it tightly.

"Let's just make this quick." My eyes find his—the same set of green eyes that left me frozen in McDowell's just weeks ago.

His eyes continue to shift from me to the stairs, beginning to panic. I know I'm wasting precious seconds. But I need him to hear me.

"I really thought that there was no kindness greater for her than death," I say, "but you showed me that we can hope for better than survival."

"Me? What... What did I do?"

"You've helped me to find myself. I'm a fighter. I can't take away another woman's chance to feel that."

Adam nods, then gets to work tying the man's arms and legs together. The knife shakes in my hand as I clench it, staring at the man and willing him to open his eyes. The pale, flickering light of the television casts the room in alternating tones. We smile at one another as we tower over him, waiting for him to wake up. In that moment, I'm aware that no two people have ever truly understood and accepted the darkness that lies within each other quite like we do.

Acknowledgements

Thanks to my editor, Joey Powell, for his incredible help and championing *Hiding Lies*, and to my publisher Mad Axe Media. Thanks to my partner, Ken, who encouraged me every step of the way to keep writing this book and being my first reader and forever number one fan. I love you. Thank you to my sister, Rachel, who sees the good in me even when I don't, and to my three cats and dog who provided endless snuggles while I typed and edited away.

The following books proved vital to me during the writing of this novel: *The Silence of the Lambs* by Thomas Harris, *Red Dragon* by Thomas Harris, *Sharp Objects* by Gillian Flynn, *You* by Caroline Kepnes, *Mindhunter* by John E. Douglas, *I'll Be Gone in the Dark* by Michelle McNamara, *My Lovely Wife* by Samantha Downing, and *The Butterfly Garden* by Dot Hutchison.

Thank you to the booksellers and librarians who support indie authors and worked incredibly hard to spread the word about my debut novel. And thank you, readers, the ones who decided to take a chance on a debut novel and author and talking about them. Without you, none of this would be possible. Thank you for reading this story.

Milton Keynes UK
Ingram Content Group UK Ltd.
UKHW020822231024
450026UK00004B/346

9 798989 173020